MW01659833

Praise for Marie Treanor's *The Devil and Via*

"Marie Treanor can always be counted on to deliver something that is different from the rest, and The Devil And Via is another such story... a gripping paranormal romantic suspense."

~ *Mrs Giggles, mrsgiggles.com*

"I read The Devil and Via from cover to cover without stopping, forgetting my reality because I was so enraptured with the tale... Plenty of action, character, and plot twists and turns... an unexpected romance; a sense of humour that is subtle yet engaging; and a satisfying outcome."

~ *Frost, Two Lips Reviews*

Look for these titles by
Marie Treanor

Now Available:

Killing Joe

Gothic Dragon

Ariadne's Thread

The Devil and Via

Queen's Gambit

Requiem for Rab

Cinderella Unmasked

(with Bonnie Dee)

The Devil and Via

Marie Treanor

A Samhain Publishing, Ltd. publication.

Samhain Publishing, Ltd.
577 Mulberry Street, Suite 1520
Macon, GA 31201
www.samhainpublishing.com

The Devil and Via

Print ISBN: 978-1-60504-427-9
Digital ISBN: 987-1-60504-350-0

Editing by Linda Ingmanson
Cover by Angie Waters

First Samhain Publishing, Ltd. electronic publication: January 2009
First Samhain Publishing, Ltd. print publication: November 2009

Dedication

To Linda, who has contributed so much to this book.

Prologue

The girl knew she was going to die. She'd given up hope of anything else. Her abused body, in its white sacrificial robes, was tied to two crossed pieces of wood, so that she couldn't move more than her head. Her ears were choked with the chanting of the dark-robed figures dancing before her, their white, inhuman faces lit grotesquely by the unforgiving beams of car headlights. It was impossible to remember now that she knew some of them, that most of them were no older than her. Something—someone—purely evil had turned all those young people, little more than children, into callous monsters happy to kill one of their own for some obscure gain.

The girl knew their gain would be very little. It was he, the older one in his black, hooded robe standing so still in front of her, who would greedily steal all she had. It was he who had changed these kids from weird teenagers into murderers. Her mind acknowledged this with curious detachment. She couldn't even feel afraid or sad or angry anymore that her life was about to be cut off so prematurely. She just wanted it over. She wanted it to stop and never happen again.

Taking a huge, deep breath, she hurled her mind as far from her as it could go, using every last gasp of strength in her body and will to tell the world what was being done to her, what was going on under the noses of her own friendly, charming people.

Someone must hear, someone must tell and stop it. Stop him...

He was strong already, she thought, as he turned quickly toward her. He had sensed the movement, the broadcast of her mind, even if he couldn't read it. Well, she could read his. With her death, he would take her gifts, make it twice as hard for whoever followed her—and she knew there would be others. He wouldn't stop now...

The chanting reached some kind of crescendo. It was his moment. Through the dark tunnel of the cowl, she saw his teeth gleam briefly. Then his hand rose. The big silver knife flashed in the headlights and drove straight into her heart.

Several hundred miles away, in a quiet village on the east coast of Scotland, Via sat bolt upright in bed, panting. Sweat trickled down between her breasts. Her heart was drumming like a rabbit's. Another dream—a bad one.

With trembling hands, she pushed back her hair, frowning with the effort of concentration. It was slipping away from her already, and yet she was aware of the importance. She really had to keep this one... Someone was frightened. A girl...? Something bad was happening to her, to the world... Taking a deep breath, she slid out of bed, went to the window and tugged back the curtains.

The night was cloudy, obliterating the stars and the full moon. She could hear the patter of rain on the window and on the ground below. She could just make out the black horizon where the sea met the sky and, closer in, on the edge of the cliff, the old graveyard with its variety of flat and standing headstones and its old-fashioned crypts. Up at the edge of the promontory, where the fence now ran, a so-called witch had been executed in a sixteenth century witch-hunt, and a few years ago, a young English tourist had fallen tragically to her death.

Was that something to do with her dream? She didn't know. It had completely gone, leaving only an unpleasant sense of unease and inadequacy.

She was used to that.

Chapter One

Three months later

Via could no longer hear her pursuers. The painful rasping of her breath drowned out their angry voices and the furious trampling in the undergrowth. She crashed through invisible tree branches, tripped over roots, rolled and sprawled her way down the dark, wooded hill until a flash of light ahead distracted her.

At first she thought they'd somehow got in front of her, that she was trapped between two groups of them. Despair threatened at last. She actually fell to her knees on the hard, dry ground before the truth came to her. It was a *pair* of lights, casting parallel beams. Onto a road. It was a car's headlights!

With a sob of gratitude, she launched herself upright and forward once more, new strength forcing her exhausted body back into a run.

The vehicle moved too fast, of course. By the time she reached the road, clawing her way out of the unexpected ditch at the side, the car had already passed her. She tore after it, desperate to be seen. Astonishingly enough, she thought she could make out a lit taxi sign on its roof—surely fate, a sign of her salvation. Her legs pumped faster.

"Taxi!" she screamed at the top of her feeble, breathless voice. It was past time for caring about noise. If the taxi didn't stop for her, it would only be a matter of time until they found her...

Later, if she got through this night alive, she might laugh at the demented sight she must present, looming out of the darkness in the middle of nowhere, in torn and ridiculous garb, no doubt covered in blood, scratches and bruises, jumping up and down and waving her arms in the air while still trying to run. For now, she could think only of preventing the taxi from getting away.

Shouts from higher up the hill told her they'd seen her, but she had no time for fresh despair. The taxi was slowing, stopping, actually reversing toward her. Without another thought, she ran the last meter along the road, wrenched open the door and threw herself into the backseat, slamming the door behind her.

"Drive!" she gasped out. "*Avanti*!"

The car leapt forward obligingly. Via, peering out of the windows at the side and the back, thought she could make out her pursuers swarming down the hill. But perhaps it was a trick of the darkness on her eyes, semi-blinded now by the car's dim internal light. Blinking rapidly, Via faced the front.

The driver, as only Italian taxi drivers can, actually turned to look at her between the front seats before he reached up with one bare arm to extinguish the glow. Via had a brief, far from comforting vision of a shaven head, scarred above one ear, black eyebrows above intense, almost glaring eyes and a muscled, hairy arm with a tattoo snaking up from the wrist.

That was when she realized her total idiocy, climbing into a car with a stranger in this situation. The dreadful possibility hit her that this man could be one of them, some muscle hired to pick her up...

"Jesus," she whispered, already reaching for the door

handle again when the muscle spoke.

"Pisa okay? Or do you want to go somewhere else?"

Via paused, her fingers gripping the handle as she glanced uncertainly back at the dark figure of the driver. Another car whizzed past in the opposite direction, and by its headlights she saw her driver's eyes watching her in the mirror. They didn't look *immediately* threatening. Neither had his voice sounded violent. On the contrary, it was merely casual, its timbre deep and curiously gentle compared with what she could see of his appearance.

She swallowed. "Pisa," she agreed. "As fast as possible. Please..."

Yesterday she might have been outraged by the way he instantly slammed his foot down and roared round the corner, narrowly avoiding an oncoming truck. Tonight she was just grateful for his unquestioning cooperation.

Collapsing against the back of her seat, she concentrated on getting her breathing under control. Her whole body trembled with solid fear as well as exertion. Somehow, she still couldn't believe she had escaped. That any of this night was real...

In front of her, the taxi driver reached forward and turned up his radio. An operatic aria assailed her ears, something she recognized from an old Marx Brothers film. The memory caught at her breath with unexpected, hysterical laughter that she had to bite back so only a sound like a startled frog escaped her lips.

Again the taxi driver turned his head to look at her. His teeth gleamed briefly in the darkness. He said something about the music, but she couldn't follow the words. Her Italian wasn't good enough.

"Bene," she said doubtfully and, apparently satisfied, the

driver turned his attention back to the road, just in time to deal with the next bend.

Smiling is good, Via reassured herself. *Smiling and opera. Both good—it's going to be okay...*

But of course, it wasn't. She soon saw headlights following at a steady pace. The vehicle kept far enough behind that she couldn't make it out, no matter how often she looked, but it never tried to pass, even when the taxi driver put the fear of God into her by slowing. The other car slowed, too.

Panicked, Via leaned forward to demand why he had reduced his speed, but before she could speak, he suddenly put his foot down again, throwing her back against the seat.

"*Scusi*," he murmured.

Via closed her mouth and peered out of the window. The car behind was still there, keeping to the same distance. But at least her driver was going fast enough to lose them—surely?—when they reached Pisa...

Via tried to study him in the gloom, wondering how to phrase her question in the tiny smattering of Italian she'd managed to acquire in the last fortnight. His hands held the wheel with a deceptive casualness. He was in complete control of the car—at least when he was looking at the road. As if he heard her thoughts, he again looked round at her between the front seats.

"*Inglese?*" he asked in friendly spirit.

"Sort of," she muttered, then, "*Si*. Do you speak English?"

He glanced at the road, then back at her with a quick grin. "Sort of. You would like me to lose this car...?" He jerked his head to the road behind before turning to face the front at last. "When we get to Pisa."

Via closed her mouth. Well, that took care of one difficulty.

She swallowed. "Yes, please."

"Okay." One hand came off the wheel to scratch absently at his leg. Bare leg, she noted. Like most younger men here in July, he wore shorts. Anything else was unbearable in the heat of the day. "So where do you want to go?" he asked. "After we lose them. You want the police?"

"No," Via said quickly. "Not the police." She wasn't quite sure why. She just knew she needed to think it out for herself before she involved the law. And the police were unlikely to believe a word of it, even supposing she could make herself understood...

She took a deep breath. "Do you know the Hotel Piccolo? Can you take me there?"

He nodded. "Of course."

The lights of the city's suburbs were close now. She hadn't long to make up her mind what to do. Her gaze fell back to the driver's profile, all clean, uncompromisingly hard lines. Yet the man had stopped for her, although she must seem to him like a mad woman, and he was being kind. He'd offered to take her to the police.

She blurted, "Do you know any other decent hotels in Pisa?"

"Of course," he said again.

"Then can you wait for me at the Piccolo, and take me to one, please?"

"Sure."

Via sat back in relief. It *would* be all right. It would...

At the first set of traffic lights, her driver turned right, then right again, roaring off around a tight bend and cutting up side streets so quickly that Via felt more disoriented than ever. They were soon the only car on the road, and by the time they entered the old city walls, lit up to be welcoming instead of threatening against the night sky, she was sure they'd lost her pursuers. Now she could worry about who was in front, waiting.

"Hotel Piccolo," said the driver, slowing and indicating to turn right under the arch into the hotel's carpark.

"No, no. Please, park round the corner—just in case they drive past and recognize your car."

Without complaint—which she more than half expected—the man pulled back into the road and drove around the corner, eventually squeezing his taxi into a tiny space outside a restaurant which had closed for the night.

"Thanks," Via muttered. "I won't be long."

As she wrenched open the car door, she heard him say casually, "Do you want any help?"

"No. No, thank you." She paused with one foot on the pavement to glance at him. "I'm...sorry to involve you in this," she said awkwardly. "You've been very kind."

And she scrambled out of the car, slamming the door and running toward the hotel entrance. For the first time she was grateful it was so late. No one except a few drunken tourists was around to witness her odd appearance. There was only, she thought as she crossed the carpark opening, the reception staff to face on her way up. Surely she could take the time to pull on a pair of jeans and a T-shirt before she had to do anything formal like check out?

Already planning how to clear her room fastest, she didn't see the shadow in the carpark archway until it moved, and hands that were only too solid yanked her into the gloom. Startlement made her cry out, though it emerged more as a grunt than a scream for help. But her body was still full of the earlier evening's adrenalin and from somewhere she found the strength and speed to spin herself out of her captor's hold, backing away until she hit the far wall of the archway.

Two men faced her. Well, two boys. They could have been only eighteen at the most, but she already knew their strength.

"You shouldn't have run away," one mocked in slow Italian so she could understand him. "As you see, it makes no difference..."

"If it pissed you people off, that's difference enough for me," she retorted. She could never shut up, never control the flapping of her mouth, even to save her life. Though in this case, she seriously doubted sweet-talking would have done any good. If there were any truly evil people in the world, she reckoned she was looking at two of them.

"You'll have to be punished," the first one sneered, moving in on her. The other came, too. The only possible escape was farther into the carpark, so she slid along the wall as they came, taking their time deliberately, she knew, to savor her fear. Only as she coiled to run did one speak with grotesquely playful warning, letting his knife glint in the carpark's wall lights.

"You want another game of tag with us? I don't think so."

Via stilled. She knew how he threw a knife. Her robe still had the bloodstains. *Is this it then?* she thought desperately, furiously. *After all I've done, breaking free and running through that damned wood, tearing my skin to bits on branches, bruising my already battered body tumbling down hills and ditches, falling in with the amiable taxi driver, just to finish up back where I started? Can life really be that unfair?*

Oh, yes.

They were closing in again, and this time she knew there was no hope. She could be killed or injured running away, or she could be killed later. Which was preferable? One way or another, she would die.

The second boy spoke—urgently, but not to her. Both looked through the archway toward the road. Someone was strolling through it. A man in shorts. The boy quickly hid his knife. Seizing every chance, as she seemed to have been doing forever, Via prepared to move with the newcomer, to use him as her protection...although would the boys care? Would they not just as happily kill this total stranger if they thought they could?

The possibility chilled her, kept her silent and still against the wall. The newcomer kept walking until he came into the light and, with astonishment, Via recognized her taxi driver.

Upright, he was a big man, imposing even in his casual shorts and loose shirt, with the lamp light glistening on his shaven head, catching the blue and orange of the winding tattoos. He kept his eyes on the boys but continued moving with deliberation, arms loose by his sides, until he stood with Via.

Dazed and unable to see him now without turning, Via looked instead at the boys. Something had changed. The odds, as it were, had evened. The boys didn't just accept that. Staring at the older man, they clearly feared it. There was a moment, only a heartbeat, of unspeakable, silent tension. Then, without a word, the first boy pulled the arm of the second and they ran through the arch into the street, their footsteps echoing round the stone walls.

Numb, all Via could feel was her thundering pulse, the shaking of her feeble legs.

"Little shit," observed the taxi driver, and abruptly it made sense to Via.

"You know one of them. That's why they were afraid!"

The driver shrugged. "I went to school with his brother. Come on, let's get your things."

This time it never entered her head to forbid him to accompany her. Though he didn't touch her, even brush against her, his mere presence was suddenly so overwhelmingly comforting that she wanted to cry. Except there was no time for that.

With casual courtesy, he held the hotel door open for her, just as if she wasn't dressed in torn, ridiculous white robes and running away from a bunch of kids. The young man at reception stared at her, his mouth hanging open.

In her best, dignified Italian, Via told him she would be checking out in a few minutes and to please have her bill prepared. Then she sailed as regally as she could toward the stairs. She heard the driver speaking in rapid Italian to the receptionist, and then he was striding beside her up the stairs, taking them two at a time.

Only when she slid the key into the lock did he touch her. Unexpectedly, his hand closed over hers, rough and warm, but when her gaze flew to his for explanation, he only murmured "*Scusi.*" Obediently, she slid her hand free and stepped back. He opened the door and moved inside, scanning the room before standing aside for her to enter.

It struck her that he, at least, was taking her danger seriously—and that without any explanation. His kindness made her want to cry. Again.

Instead, while he shut the door and leaned against it, she whisked around the room without looking at him, throwing things into her small suitcase, except for her jeans and a loose T-shirt, which she cast on the bed until the rest was done. Only when she bolted the bathroom door to change did it strike her she'd let a strange man into her hotel room. For some reason, it didn't matter.

With her still-shaking hands, she peeled off the torn

robes—ignoring, after the briefest examination, all the blood and the bruises—and pulled on her fresh clothes. As a concession to cleanliness, she splashed water onto her aching face, patting it dry with a towel as she emerged from the bathroom.

He stood where she'd left him, leaning against the door. She thought he'd been gazing out of the window through the open shutters, but now his eyes came back to her and for one moment she met his steady gaze. Something twisted inside her, somewhere in the region of her stomach. It wasn't unpleasant, but then neither was he.

In full light, the hard lines and planes of his face looked somehow more refined, the shiny baldness more Yule Brynner than skin-head. The fact that she couldn't see the troubling scar from this angle helped, too. His eyebrows, though thick and black, were well-shaped, almost sculpted in appearance above intense, almond-shaped brown eyes. Crow's feet of laughter spanned outwards from the corners of his eyes, and his *lips*, well...

Her breath caught. She swung away from his steady gaze only to meet her own in the impersonal dressing table mirror.

"Oh *bugger*," she said furiously. One cheek was swollen and dark. A black eye was forming nicely, and the corner of her lip was split. Her forehead and cheeks were covered in scratches from the tree branches, and her hair was wild and tangled. What a mess! And a timely reminder that her eccentrically attractive taxi driver was unlikely to reciprocate her unexpected interest.

Rueful laughter caught in her throat.

"It must hurt," he observed.

"Tomorrow it will. Tonight I can't seem to feel anything."

"Shock," he explained.

She glanced up at him. "I haven't thanked you properly. You didn't need to..."

"Neither do you," he interrupted. "Are you ready?"

"Yes," she sighed, dragging a comb through her hair before throwing it into her handbag. She grabbed her case and walked toward the door.

As she approached, he brushed past her to the bathroom. Via watched him, frowning, her hand impatiently on the latch. An instant later he re-emerged with the torn robes rolled up in one hand.

"I don't want that," she said harshly. "Just stick it in the bin."

He shrugged, but kept the robes as he followed her out of the room. In the corridor, he wordlessly took the case from her, despite her protest that it wasn't heavy and she could manage easily, and strode off down the stairs.

Rather to her surprise, the bill was ready for her at reception and it took only a few moments to escape into the night. Via looked round with a fearfulness she was beginning to find rather pathetic in herself, not to say annoying. And yet, when the taxi driver walked beside her, large and loose-limbed, her fears instantly calmed. He'd saved her too often, she thought ruefully. She was dependent on someone she'd never met before tonight and would never see again.

Since this rather disturbing idea was nevertheless considerably more pleasant than any others which had sprung out of the night's events, she stuck with it during the short walk to the taxi, mulling it over in a tired, muddled sort of a way. It was all her brain seemed capable of right now. When they reached the taxi, she climbed without thought into the front seat.

If the driver noticed this subtle change in their relationship, he gave no sign. He merely tossed her case into the back and slid into the seat beside her. She found herself gazing at his strong, bare thighs, at the scattering of black hairs and the play of muscle as he twisted to put on his belt. She watched his capable hands, one resting on the gear lever, the other slipping the key into the ignition. Just for an instant, she imagined those big hands on her skin, the rough tips of his long fingers brushing across her nipples. Then, shocked at herself, she glanced up to his face, to check if he'd somehow guessed her wayward thoughts.

The steady brown eyes were on hers. Her stomach lurched with embarrassment and something else she couldn't think about. She felt the hot blood sweep through her body to her face, but the driver didn't seem to notice.

It was just a trick of her mind, translating this sudden dependence on her saviour into sexual attraction. It wasn't real. He wasn't her type. Was he?

He asked, "Did you come to Italy alone?"

Via blinked. "What? Yes. Why?"

"Is there not someone here who can look after you?"

Surprise brought unsteady laughter. "Apart from you?" Something changed in his eyes at that, and she looked away, suddenly conscious of how her words might be misinterpreted. "I'm fine. I came alone because I came to work."

He turned the key in the ignition. "As what?"

"Someone was foolish enough to pay me to teach English to their children."

He glanced at her, even while coaxing his car out of its minute parking space. "Yes? You've been here long?"

"Two weeks. The children are not really children—they're going to university to study English, and I was hired to converse with them in English for a fortnight. During which time I earned enough to stay for another week or so, which I had planned to do…"

The taxi pulled out into the road. "This family is friendly? Can you go to them?"

"Oh, no." There was a short silence. She felt his gaze on her and itched to point his attention back to the road.

After a moment, he said, "Hotel, then."

"Yes, please," said Via, and was appalled by how small and lost her voice sounded. *Not now, I will not cry now…*

Unexpectedly, his right hand lifted off the wheel and moved to brush against her cheek. His fingertips felt rough, yet his touch was curiously gentle, brief and feather-light and clearly meant to comfort. There was nothing to cause her gasp, yet she couldn't prevent it. Perversely, his attention stayed on the road during the short caress, and Via found herself grateful for it. She felt herself falling apart.

After a short silence, the taxi driver spoke again, carefully, as if he'd worked out the English in his head first.

"If the boys at the Piccolo are connected to what happened to you earlier, I think you are safe now."

Via frowned at his averted face. "Why?" she demanded, afraid to give in to this hope. "Because you recognized one of them?"

He nodded at the road, but by then another less acceptable thought had struck Via with all the force of a hammer. "No, wait," she exclaimed. "It means rather that *you* are in danger now, too! These people have no conscience."

But the taxi driver's face only dissolved into a spontaneous grin. The crow's feet at the corners of his eyes crinkled disarmingly as he turned the full force of his smile on her.

Warmth spread through her body, soothing the last trembles in her limbs.

"For me, no danger," he assured her before turning back to the road in time to turn left through a red light. Fortunately, traffic was quiet.

"Because you know his brother?" Via asked doubtfully.

"Yes... This is a small city. Word travels fast. Hotel Leonardo," he added, pointing across the street. "Do you want to try there first?"

"Try there first" sounded rather daunting, but this *was* the busiest time of the year for hotels...

"Sure. It looks a nice place." It did, too, an old, yellow building on a quiet street. She had no idea where she was in relation to anywhere else, but right now that was a minor concern.

Chapter Two

The hotel foyer was empty when they entered, although from a doorway on the right came the sounds of cheerful voices chattering over some bland, understated music. The hotel bar, she presumed.

Via wandered over to the deserted desk. The driver put her case down beside her and began to walk toward the voices. It bothered Via that she was letting him do this for her. She was not so incapable. It was just, now that she'd finally stopped shaking, she felt so damned tired...

Before he'd even reached the bar door, a man in long trousers and an open-necked shirt came out and saw him. Abruptly, the slightly harassed-looking face lit up with what looked like amazement as well as pleasure.

"*Ciao!* Giancarlo!" he exclaimed, striding to meet the driver with hand held out. The driver grinned back, shaking the offered hand. A rapid exchange in Italian followed that Via didn't even try to understand, though a second later they both glanced over at her. The hotelier greeted her politely, said something else to the driver, who punched him lightly on the arm, and then they both moved to join her at the desk.

Still talking, the hotelier consulted his computer screen, clicking here and there until eventually his mouth closed and he looked expectantly at Via. Leaning against the desk, heavy-eyed, she'd felt herself beginning to nod off to the melodious sounds of their voices and hadn't heard a word. Wildly, she looked round at the taxi driver, who, with a trace of amusement in his dark eyes, explained, "Federico says he has a good room you can have tonight, but someone is booked into it for tomorrow. You would have to move into a much smaller room with a view of next door's wall if you wanted to stay longer."

"I just need it for tonight. I love his room," Via said, thinking of any bed with deep longing.

And in fact, it was a lovely room. Spacious and furnished with old-fashioned, dark wood furniture, it contained two single beds and had a delightful view over the river and the bridges.

"I think," Via said, turning her back on the window to face the taxi driver, who was laying her case down on the nearest bed, "I think I have double cause to be grateful for the people you know. Thank you."

He only nodded, then lifted his gaze to her face. "You should report what happened to the police."

"Not tonight," she pleaded. "I can't face it tonight."

"In the morning, then. You are quite safe now, you know."

"I know."

He has the most amazing eyes, Via thought irrelevantly. *You could drown in them so happily...* Then his gaze shifted, slipping down to her mouth, and her heart lurched. But of course he was only looking at her split lip. *Get over it, V...!* His gaze came back to hers only an instant later. With a faint, slightly twisted smile, he turned away, heading for the door.

Panic shot through her like an arrow. He was leaving. Already! She really didn't want him to go, and the strength of that desire shook her—not least because she recognized even through her confusion that it wasn't all to do with her inevitable fear of being alone.

"Wait," she exclaimed, starting after him. He turned at once, and she stopped, casting around for a reason to make him stay just a few minutes longer. "I—we... I—I haven't paid you."

For a moment he looked completely blank, as if he had no idea what she was talking about. Then the breath hissed out between his teeth. He said, "I'm sorry, I can't take money from you."

Frowning, Via looked up from her purse, where she was rummaging for euros. "Why not?" she demanded. Over the distance between them, his eyes seemed to search hers for a moment. Then his lips twisted.

"But you could buy me coffee downstairs, if it makes you feel better."

Via smiled. "Okay," she said with heavy relief. And yet her heart had begun to beat strongly in her breast, and she had no more idea of sleeping.

"*Ciao*, Giancarlo!" cried the barmaid when they approached. Young with big, blond hair and suspiciously dark, long eyelashes, she reached over the bar to grab him by the head and kiss his lips smackingly. There was a huge smile on her own lips. Jealously, Via saw him laugh and hug her back. She realized she knew nothing about him. He could be married to the barmaid with six kids and three mistresses. Although she wasn't sure taxi driving would finance such an extravagant lifestyle...

Somewhere in the conversation, drinks were clearly ordered because, still talking, the barmaid produced a glass of orange juice and another of red wine. Plonking them on the bar, she grinned at Via and waved them both toward a table.

"She'll bring the coffee," the taxi driver—Giancarlo, she

couldn't doubt—explained, carrying the drinks to a table by the window.

Maybe it was a form of shock, but as he slid onto the sofa beside her, Via was conscious of a new excitement. More than comfort radiated from the large, loose-limbed frame of her gallant taxi driver. He had a *presence*, and Via realized suddenly that that alone would have scared off the lads at the Piccolo, whether or not they'd recognized him. And it was a presence she enjoyed being close to, with the sort of enjoyment that wanted more. She wanted to put her hand on his bare knee, press her leg against his muscled thigh.

She took a gulp of wine instead.

"Where in England are you from, Vittoria?"

Via felt her eyes widening. "How do you know my name?"

His black eyebrows lifted. "I read it on your passport when you registered."

"Oh. Well, no one calls me Victoria anymore. I'm Via."

"Via?" He smiled, sending a new flock of butterflies dancing in her stomach. "The Way," he translated. "How did that happen?"

She opened her mouth to tell the usual lie, then suddenly found herself saying ruefully, "It was an accident from early days at school. I found it hard to write, and my name took forever, so I cheated. After the first two letters, I skipped to the last and the teacher thought it was my pet name at home. I've been Via ever since."

He was still looking at her expectantly, so she babbled on. "And I'm not from England at all. I'm from Scotland."

"I thought your accent was different. So, what made you come here for so short a job?"

Via shrugged. "I got sacked from my old one."

"I'm sorry."

"Don't be—I hated it anyway. The worst thing about whisky-bottling plants is that no matter how much you like whisky when you start, after a month you can't even look at the stuff."

"You're losing me," he said, the crow's feet crinkling attractively round his amused eyes. "Too fast."

"Sorry. I was glad to get rid of my old job because I was bored, wanted to do something else."

"What?"

Via sighed. "Not sure yet. Maybe teach, only I don't have the qualifications. You can see why this job in Italy was so timely for me."

He stirred. His thigh brushed against hers, and the tingly warmth from it spread through her whole body. He asked, "How did you get it?"

"A neighbor of my family is an Italian businessman. When he heard I'd been fired, he told me about friends of his in Pisa who wanted a native English speaker to brush up their sons' conversation. I jumped at it. A couple of weeks being shown the sights, followed by at least another week on my own, doing what I wanted..."

"But it didn't work out like that?"

"Well, at first it did. The Marinuzzis were very kind, met me at the airport, drove me to the hotel, invited me for lunch every day, and dinner more often than not. The boys took me around, were very polite and respectful, if not friendly, precisely. In fact, it crossed my mind more than once that they were acting and didn't think very much of me at all. A teenage thing. As if I was more their parents' generation than theirs, you know?"

Giancarlo nodded. Since he still looked interested, and Via

was finding it hard to stop now she'd started, she went on. "But their English was very good. I'm not sure they gained anything from my expensive appointment. Anyway, on my final day, I was quite surprised when they invited me out with their friends. I thought their parents had put them up to it, so I went along. The twins—did I tell you they were twins?—drove, but they didn't take me to a restaurant or even a bar. We went outside the city, to some ruin on a hill and they...they..."

Abruptly, the clenched hand in her lap was covered in his. Almost with wonder, she felt his fingers grip strongly, bringing a secret excitement as well as warmth and fresh courage. Looking at their hands, she said more steadily, "They tied me up and shut me in a cave until their friends came. Then they came back and...and stripped me. I fought them. I thought...I thought they were going to rape me."

His fingers tightened convulsively on hers, causing a quick smile of gratitude to flicker across her lips. "They didn't," she reassured him, still evading eye contact. "Though I think they meant to later...They put that stupid robe on me and dragged me back to the ruins. I think it had been a church. They tied me to a sort of inverted cross."

She felt his hand twitch and at last looked up to meet his frowning gaze. "They were holding some sort of Black Mass," she said. "A Satanic ritual. They were dressed in black robes, heavily hooded for the most part so I couldn't see their faces, calling on Satan, chanting stuff I couldn't understand except a few words of it. Some of it was Latin. Most of the kids were fu—having sex with each other, indiscriminately, changing partners, two or even three partners at once. An orgy, I suppose. The twins were in there; so were the boys we saw at the Piccolo. But someone older was in charge of them, keeping them away from me, except when he ordered one or the other of them to...cut me, or...or touch me. One of them, the boy from the Piccolo, threw a knife into my side. Some sort of parody of Christ's thing... Don't worry, it only nicked my skin. I checked in the bathroom when I changed... Anyway, it was clear that the climax to all this, if you'll pardon the expression, was to be my 'sacrifice' to Satan."

Via snorted and took another sip of wine. It was relaxing her, making it easy to tell the nightmarish tale—at least in outline. Giancarlo said nothing. His serious eyes gazed steadily into hers, taking in every word of her story—or at least, she supposed, as much as his grasp of her English would allow. But at least he showed no signs of doubting her.

Without meaning to, she blurted, "Do you know the really funny thing? I never believed such nonsensical things went on outside the pages of my dad's old Dennis Wheatley novels. Yet it was almost as if I'd been there before, seen it all before..."

Frowning with concentration, Via tried and failed to retrieve the memory. All she had was tonight's living nightmare. And coffee with this kind man who would now think she was completely mad.

He asked, "How did you escape?"

She shrugged. "I pretended to be so overcome with fear—not a great test of acting, I assure you—that I fainted. Then, when they took me down from the cross to ready me for my ritual murder, or rape, I don't know, I kneed the old man in the balls and pushed him into the others. Then I ran like hell. They chased me all through that wood and down the hill to the road where you stopped for me."

Via looked away. "You see why I'm doubtful about the police. Who would believe *that*? I'd just be dubbed a hysterical woman with morbid sexual fantasies."

"I don't think so."

Her eyes widened, swinging back to his.

He said, "This is not such a rare event in Italy. The police are very aware of these so-called devil-worshippers. We had a wake-up call a few years ago, when members of a rock band began murdering one another in their rituals."

"Seriously?"

"Seriously. Mostly they are just confused, alienated kids living out sick fantasies, but they are taken as a serious threat in our society. Even the priests are taught special courses on it now, to try to understand and help. To be honest, I think you had a very lucky escape. Others will not be so lucky."

Her heart quailed. She felt cornered and furious.

"But this is different," she objected. "Someone was encouraging, *controlling* these young people."

"The police need to know that, too."

There was no way round it now. Resigned, she said, "I'll tell them in the morning. Where should I go? The local Carabinieri office?"

"Yes. Or I can phone them for you and get someone who speaks English to come here to see you."

She smiled. "Can you really do that?"

His eyes smiled into hers. "I can do anything."

Her breath caught again. Was he *flirting* with her? Suddenly she remembered her hand in his, burning into her leg. She laughed unsteadily. "I know you can," she said with feeling. At which point the barmaid brought the coffee, and he said something teasing to her, too, and Via realized that, of course, it was just his manner and the fact he felt sorry for her.

To cover her embarrassment, she drew her hand free and rummaged inside her bag for her worn and much-scribbled-on map of Pisa. Spreading it out on the table between them, she reached for the strong espresso and took a sip, sighing in thoughtless appreciation.

"You like Italian coffee? I should have asked you before ordering."

"I love Italian coffee," she assured him. "Can you show me on this map where we are? This hotel?"

"Sure." He bent over it, dragging a pen from his back pocket and stabbing it immediately on a marked road near the river. "Just here." He carefully made a cross between the scribbles that made sense only to her. "And in case the Carabinieri don't come to you, their office is *here.*"

Via, who hadn't been looking at the map at all but at his fascinating face, was caught suddenly by his intense, dark gaze when he glanced up at her and found her staring. His eyebrow twitched.

"What?" he asked, smiling.

"Nothing." Via flushed. "I…I have a problem with directions. That's why I don't drive. And another reason I don't really want to face the police—I'd never be able to explain where it happened and…"

"Hey, Giancarlo!" someone called across the room—a young man hurrying toward the door, grinning and waving to them. "*Ciao*!"

"*Ciao*, Enrico," Giancarlo returned. Via didn't know whether she felt more relief or annoyance at the loss of his attention. She was too tired and confused. She wanted him to touch her, yet she was so afraid he would. Everything that had happened that night pressed in on her, churning her up, centering all her too intense emotions on *him*. For some reason, she liked it, but she didn't trust it.

She said quickly, "I have to go to bed and let you return to your life," and began stuffing the map back into her bag. He was silent, just watching her until at last she put her bag down on the table and lifted her gaze to his. "I'll never forget what you did for me. Thank you."

He smiled, nudging her lightly with his shoulder. "I did nothing. Just there at the right time. Come, I'll walk you to your room and leave you."

Her heart hammered as she walked silently upstairs beside him. What did he mean? Why would he walk her to her room, if he meant to leave her there? Was he just giving her the chance to say no? *Touch me, please touch me—take my hand, anything...*

He was simply being kind, keeping her company until the safety of her room. She was in no condition to attract anyone. *But if he were to kiss me, what would it be like...?*

Sore—Marco split your lip, remember?

They were in the empty upstairs hall now, walking the last few steps to her door. *Why doesn't he even speak?*

Why don't you, *Via?*

"Well, this is me," she blurted inanely. "Thank you for everything. I really am..."

"Stop thanking me," he interrupted, grasping her wrist at last and giving it a little admonitory shake as they came to a halt outside her door. Fortunately, he seemed more amused than annoyed. "Believe it or not, I am glad to know you."

She smiled at that. "*Ciao*, Giancarlo," she mocked. His fingers slid down to take her hand properly. The expression in his deep, dark eyes was unreadable yet so enticing that she reached her free hand to his shoulder and stood on tiptoe to kiss his cheek. At once, his arm came round her in a quick hug.

Her face ached with unshed tears and she threw her arm around his neck, embracing him convulsively. She felt his other arm come up to hold her, too. His cheek pressed on her hair.

Surreptitiously, she wiped her eyes on his shirt.

And then, just as she was about to pull back and apologize, she realized with shock that his erection was pressing into her abdomen.

Oh Jesus, he does want me!

Now what do I do?

Kiss him, ask him to stay!

I can't, I'm not ready for this, I don't know *him…*

God, I want him!

How could she not? His big body felt so good in her arms, warm and hard, his hold at once strong and gentle, seeming to promise everything she had ever wanted in a lover. Between her legs, she was wet, wetter than she could ever remember, without so much as a kiss. And she was shaking again.

When he lifted his head from her hair, pushing up her chin with his fingers, she saw with awe that the intriguing, unreadable expression in his eyes had always been at least part lust. Now they were heavy and clouded with it. They were predatory, devouring her, scalding her with their heat. And God, her body burned in excited response.

Say the words, V. Make him stay, don't lose this chance…

She stared up at him, desperate and terrified. Somewhere behind the desire, or maybe part of it, she thought she saw *anguish* in his eyes.

Kiss me! For God's sake, kiss me—don't make me *kiss* you.

Still, apart from the rapid rise and fall of his breathing, he didn't move, just roved his hot gaze over her eyes and lips and throat. How could she be so afraid of this stranger's touch and still want it so badly? She knew, with the tiny part of her head that could still think, that her desire was all muddled up with shock, with fear of being alone, with gratitude. She knew that right now she was just a walking, breathing mass of emotion. But there was something about him, some wild, powerful passion she was dying to taste. *Make your mind up, Victoria! Do it!*

Abruptly, before her courage failed, she stood on tiptoe once more, reaching with her mouth for his.

"Sh-sh." His hand came up quickly, one finger on her parted lips. His voice was a low, husky whisper. "If I kiss you, I won't stop."

Then don't stop. Delicious, terrifying thought.

His finger stroked along her lower lip and slid down her chin to her throat, making her shiver, until it gently pushed her hair behind her shoulder. "You are too beautiful and too hurt. And I am too…needy."

His lips twitched. "*Buona notte, carissima.*" His head swooped down. Her stomach lurched in mingled panic and longing. But his lips only brushed against hers for the tiniest instant. And then his lips and hands left her, and he strode quickly along the corridor toward the stairs. She had time to admire the motion of his tight buttocks in his shorts before she turned away with a shuddering breath that was at least part laughter—a very small part—and let herself into the room. Alone.

Arturo Marinuzzi had two studies, each very different from the other. The outer one, where he occasionally received honored guests, was a bright, spacious room looking onto the garden. Spotlessly clean and neat, it boasted a large, antique desk of inlaid rosewood, two leather armchairs and three large, tall matching bookcases full of reference books, political biographies and works on national and international trade law, all arranged tidily by subject and author. A blue Persian rug added warmth to the otherwise stark décor.

Marinuzzi liked this room, but it was in his inner sanctum he chose to wait for news, partly because he wanted to look things up, and partly because he was furiously angry and wanted to storm. Both activities he preferred to conduct away from prying eyes, namely his wife's. The inner study was small, crowded, dark. The one tiny window was permanently shuttered. And there was only one hard wooden chair, piled with old and dusty books. No one cleaned in here. Both Marinuzzi's wife and his housekeeper thought it was a cupboard. He never disabused them of this belief and kept the door locked at all times, whichever side of it he was on.

Now, waiting for the twins to come back, he paced round the room, unable even to research his next step until he knew what had happened. He'd had a bad feeling about that Scottish girl ever since she'd first arrived. Easy enough on the eyes and ears, she'd seemed neither over-educated nor particularly gifted. Now he seriously doubted she was worth even the money he'd paid her to instruct his sons, never mind anything else.

The pacing wasn't helping either the sick feeling in his gut or the pain in his groin, but he kept it up anyway until finally he heard the sound he'd been waiting for, the opening of the outer study door. He limped to the door and unlocked it. Already he could hear the boys talking, all four of them at once, arguing more and more loudly as to whose fault it was.

"Be quiet," Marinuzzi said, entering the room and closing and locking the door before he deigned to look at any of them. Total silence surrounded him. At last, turning, he gazed at his eldest, Giovanni, who was scowling. Not a good sign. Generally he hated to mar his handsome brow. Marinuzzi sighed. "Well?"

"She got in a taxi," Giovanni blurted.

Marinuzzi stared. "She got in a taxi? On that road? For God

sake, did she have the forethought to call one before she left Pisa, or did one of you kindly lend her your cell phone?"

All four of them squirmed under his sarcasm. His own boys were distinctly wary, but it was the other two thugs who looked terrified. Even more ominous. In spite of his self-belief, Marinuzzi's gut twisted.

"It was just luck," Matteo said. "It happened to be passing and it picked her up."

"And you just waved her off? Get to that flea-pit of a hotel and bring her back!"

"We tried that," Matteo said. "Or at least Marco and Benito did." Although Matteo always sounded reasonable and calm, there was clearly a certain pleasure as well as relief in being able to pass the buck.

Marinuzzi's glance at the other two boys was quick and piercing before he said, "Something tells me she's not waiting in the drawing room."

"The taxi driver was with her." Matteo again excused his friends. Marinuzzi ignored him, continuing to glare at Benito and Marco, who shuffled their feet.

"At least, we thought it was the driver, only I know him, and he isn't," Benito offered.

"You're not making any sense," Marinuzzi said.

"He's Carabinieri."

There was silence. Marinuzzi could hear his own even breathing as well as the nervous panting of the boys.

"Worse," Marco said, "he's Special Operations. And a captain. We could have taken him out and grabbed the girl, but we thought involving the police would bring too much attention."

Marinuzzi swung away.

"It would. You were right."

Though the boys' visible sags of relief were not lost on Marinuzzi, his mind was dealing with far more important things.

"So what," he murmured, "was a high-ranking Special Operations officer doing anywhere near her? Was he driving the taxi that picked her up? If he had men watching last night, it means there has been a security breach." His eyes narrowed, scanning all four boys. "Someone has blabbed."

"No!" Benito exclaimed, bringing the cold, piercing eyes back to him with enough force to make him tremble. "I mean, you're right, of course, *if* he was watching, but he wasn't."

"Then what was he doing there at exactly the wrong time?" Marinuzzi enquired. "Booking a room?"

"I don't know," Benito confessed. "But I called my brother to find out, and he says Giancarlo, the officer, is still on long-term sick leave."

Well, that was something. If the officer had interfered by chance, acting from misplaced gallantry rather than a planned operation, then perhaps they'd lost nothing.

"Should we go back and get her later?" Giovanni asked. "First light?"

"No." He turned back to face the boys. "Forget her. As it stands now, I seriously doubt there will be any more trouble from her. She was clearly terrified, probably too scared to speak out. I expect her simply to go home now, as fast as she can leave Italy, and we'll hear no more. However, I'll check on this policeman. His name?"

"Di Ripoli. Giancarlo Di Ripoli."

"All right. Go. Just remember—if by any chance the police *do* approach you, you know *nothing*. The girl can name all of you, but her story can easily be discredited. Most importantly, *my family must not be associated with this business.* Remember.

"And tomorrow, to be on the safe side, we go to the Cinque Terre."

Chapter Three

A week later, Via had no intention of going home for as long as her money would hold out.

From sheer stubborn determination, she refused to let her plans be changed by teenage thugs. Of course, Giancarlo's assurance of her safety made a difference too, but somehow she didn't want the nightmare to be her defining memory of Italy.

By a stroke of good fortune, she emerged from the Hotel Leonardo the morning after her ordeal, feeling ridiculously brave just by walking round the corner—and saw a handwritten notice in a bakery shop window advertising an apartment at very reasonable rates. The apartment turned out to be a self-contained room with a bathroom and entry on to a tiny, roof garden from which she could see out across lots of other roofs to the hills beyond the city. Via fell in love with it instantly, parted with her cash to the amiable if slightly lecherous looking baker, and returned to the hotel to collect her stuff.

There she discovered the Carabinieri waiting for her. Giancarlo had indeed got someone to come to her. Surprisingly, the interview had not been nearly as difficult as she had expected. As Giancarlo had promised, her story was both believed and taken seriously. The pleasant young man, who spoke excellent English, wrote down everything she said and at the end, asked the question the taxi driver hadn't.

"Did you recognize this older man?"

Via nodded, bringing her gaze back to his. "Arturo Marinuzzi." The policeman's brows lifted, and Via wasn't surprised. Her ex-employer was a respected and wealthy member of the community. "I didn't see his face, but I heard his voice. It's very distinctive. Cold and sort of sarcastic, even when he's only saying good morning."

The young man wrote that down, too.

Closing his file and standing, he asked, "Would you like to be taken to the hospital?"

"Do you mean for evidence?" Via asked. "I'm afraid I've showered twice."

A smile flickered across the policeman's face. "No, for your health. You look badly bruised. We should be able to get all the evidence we need from the robe you wore."

"My robe?" Via frowned. "But I left it...oh. Giancarlo gave it to you?"

There was that smile again, barely perceptible before it vanished. "*Si.* Giancarlo."

"Well, my bruises will heal, thank you. I've no need to waste a doctor's time."

And that was that. The policeman left, Via paid her bill to a careless young receptionist at the Leonardo and carried her case round the corner to the flat above the bakery. There was a private entrance through a latched gate, up a rickety staircase to the roof garden.

There, she unpacked her few clothes, then sat outside in her tiny garden in the sunshine to count her money and do the arithmetic. If she drew on her meager savings from the bottling plant, too, she reckoned she could stay two more weeks, including a little traveling, a little sight-seeing and a little shopping.

And that's what she did. She bought some new, light clothes—wispy cotton dresses, cropped trousers and tops—and some make-up to hide the blossoming bruises. She went again to the Piazza del Duomo and gazed with awe at the magnificent cathedral she'd previously seen only with her bored charges (who had turned out to be, more or less literally, the kids from hell), and managed to think of the wonderful art and architecture rather than of them. She sat on the grass of the Camposanto for a whole hour just contemplating the peculiar angle of Pisa's famous and decidedly squint tower.

She walked round the city with her map in short hops, stopping frequently in shady pavement cafés for coffee, orange juice and ice cream. She spent hours in the cafés, mostly listening to the conversations around her, even on occasion joining in with some friendly locals, until she began to pick up the pattern of the language as well as the frequently used words. She expanded her vocabulary and her acquaintance in the local shops, buying fresh pasta and vegetables and the hugest peaches she'd ever seen in her life.

One day, she got up early and took the train to Florence, where she spent an exhausting but amazing day and, with her mobile phone, took photographs of herself standing on the Ponte Vecchio. She sent them to her brothers in Scotland.

A whole week flew past in growing contentment. Gradually, she stopped scanning passersby for the teenage faces she never wanted to see again, forgot to listen for Marinuzzi's outraged voice calling her to account for her accusation. As her injuries healed, her ordeal faded from her mind like past nightmares.

Just occasionally, she found herself dwelling on the bizarre ritual, but mostly because it tugged at some other elusive memory she couldn't quite grasp. Italy was casting its spell and drowning her fears.

One early afternoon, she returned from a shopping expedition, walking across the central bridge and counting the streets opening off the main road on the other side. Picking the third, narrow street as usual, she wandered along it, enjoying the shade until she crossed a wider street and a hot beam of sunshine struck her on the shoulders. Sighing with something approaching pure happiness, Via looked around her at the Mediterranean buildings with their colored shutters, the café on the corner with a crowd of people sitting outside over some wine and remains of their lunch. It was a nice place. Via had had coffee there herself more than once. The outside tables sat under distinctive stone arches and a high, vaulted ceiling.

As her gaze drifted back to her own direction, a burst of laughter from the café drew her attention back. They were local people rather than tourists—about eight of them sitting round two tables pulled together, and now that she wasn't looking straight into the sun she could see they were youngish men and women, perhaps her own age or a little older. One of them, the man sitting with his back to the wall with his feet up on the table, looked like her taxi driver, Giancarlo.

Via's heart lurched. In a week, she'd never once laid eyes on him, even though she'd scanned all the taxis she passed. Surely, she was mistaken... She paused, taking off her sunglasses and looking straight at the man who resembled her savior.

He was gazing right at her. He smiled faintly, lifted his hand to her, and, before she could stop it, a huge smile split her own face. Acting from instinct, she turned to cross the road to him. Only then she thought, *he's with his friends, I can't intrude.* So, hastily, she waved to him and swung away, taking another few steps toward home before she realized how rude that was. She owed him more. And she had no need to intrude.

All she had to do was go up to him, say hello and thanks and how are you, and leave him to his friends.

Resolutely, she turned yet again and made her way across the road between the bicycles. Her stomach full of nervous butterflies, she was afraid to look at him in case it was clear he would rather ignore her.

However, by the time she'd plucked up the courage, he'd not only taken his feet off the table and stood, he was pushing past his grinning friends to come and meet her at the arch opposite the café door.

He was bigger than she remembered, his amazing dark eyes more intense. But in the sunlight, he looked somehow more approachable, more handsome, with his cool, shaven head and clear, fine-featured face. Today, his crumpled shorts were dark red, and with them he wore a loose white shirt that covered the bulging muscles of his shoulders and arms, and on his feet, what looked like the same pair of sandals. Jesus sandals, they used to call them.

Via smiled a little nervously, trying to cover it with a teasing, "*Ciao*, Giancarlo!"

His eyes crinkled at that. Grinning, he replied in Italian, "*Ciao*, yourself. You look lovely."

She flushed. "It's the make-up," she assured him, but he only smiled again, lifting his arm in a teasing sort of a way and gently touching his fist to the bruise on her cheek, so lightly it barely even tickled.

He said, "I thought you'd gone home."

"No. I found an apartment and enough money to stay until at least the end of next week."

"Yes?" His eyes lit up. Via remembered the feel of him in her arms that night, his erection pressing hotly into her abdomen. She smiled uncertainly.

"I'm glad to have met you again." God, she'd had a whole speech worked out, just in case she ran into him, and now that she had, she couldn't remember a bloody word of it.

"Yes? Do you want to come and have a glass of wine with us?"

Now, at least, her smile was spontaneous. "I'd love to."

It seemed quite natural, too, when he took her hand to lead her across to his friends, who stopped talking to listen to the introductions. There were two women, beautiful as only Italian women can be, all flawless olive skin, slim, graceful elegance and casually spectacular clothes. The others were darkly attractive men of Giancarlo's own age, perhaps, or a little younger. All gave her very curious looks, but they seemed happy enough to accept her presence, especially after she answered some quickly thrown question about the length of her stay, in Italian.

"You learned Italian in a week?" Giancarlo teased, lounging into the seat beside her and calling into the café for another glass.

"Well, I *improved* in a week," Via corrected. Then, more enthusiastically, "But I love your language! And your country, what I've seen of it."

While a waiter brought a glass, and Giancarlo poured her some wine, Via told him what she'd been doing with her week, punctuating it with amusing anecdotes and observations that made him smile. All the while she talked, he never seemed to take his eyes off her. Blatantly, he gave her all his attention, and it was intoxicating.

Pausing to take a sip of wine, she made a half-hearted attempt to pull herself out of whatever it was she was sinking into so fast.

"What about you?" she asked. "I gather you're not working

today?"

"I'm on leave."

"Oh." She laughed a little breathlessly. "Well, that explains it. I've been looking out for you in all the taxis."

"Ah." He leaned forward to pick up his glass. His downy arm brushed against hers, sending a frisson of pleasure shivering through her. The tattooed snake twisted up his wrist as he turned the glass in his hands. For a moment, he regarded her over his orange juice. Then he said, "Well, I've a confession to make. I'm not a taxi driver."

Via's mouth fell open. Of course he was a taxi driver! His entire persona, for her, was built on the fact that he was an ordinary taxi driver who'd stopped for her. A good Samaritan who looked like a gang leader.

Closing her lips with a snap, she repeated, "Not a taxi driver? But you were driving a taxi."

"For Lucca." He nodded across the table to a good-looking, black-haired man, who glanced up from his conversation with the glamorous girl in yellow to grin briefly. "Lucca drank too much beer and had to be put to bed, so I drove his taxi home to his father before he got kicked out of the family firm."

"Self-righteous bastard," said Lucca amiably.

Via took that in, managing to readjust enough to ask, "So what *do* you do, then?"

Giancarlo took a deep breath. "Actually," he said, "I'm a policeman."

Via blinked. The sun glinted on Giancarlo's shaven head, shooting sparks of gold through his dark brown eyes. Some serious readjustment became necessary here. Her lip twitched.

Giancarlo grinned and reached across to refill her glass.

It was a delightful afternoon. Giancarlo's friends were both welcoming and amusing, interested and interesting. There was a breathless excitement in sitting by his side, his hand or arm occasionally brushing against her, or deliberately touching her to attract her attention or to make a point. It was as if the promise of their first fraught meeting with all its complications and distractions was now being fulfilled. It had entered Via's head more than once over the last week that if she ever met her gallant taxi driver again, he would be unlikely to live up to the figure her imagination and her need had made of him. But *this*, this was someone she *liked*, someone who made her laugh and who seemed to like her. Someone whose lightest touch burned her skin and set her craving for more.

He drank only orange juice and water. Via couldn't help wondering if that was for her, to stop himself getting drunk and inane like so many men littering the path of her past. No stranger herself to drunken inanity, she felt in no danger of it here. The whole atmosphere was far too lazy for the hard-drinking sessions of home. A couple of glasses merely relaxed her, loosened her reserved tongue, gave her the confidence to try out and further improve her own Italian.

Halfway through the afternoon, she went inside the café to find the single toilet. There, in the tiny mirror, she stared into her own bright, sparkling eyes. Her cheeks were faintly flushed, betraying the pleasure and excitement she felt. Hastily, she splashed a little cold water onto them. But, with just a little smugness, she thought she looked quite good, her bruising almost gone now. She particularly liked that she seemed to amuse him, considering she'd been such a fearful mess at their first encounter.

The question was, did she have the nerve to ask him to dinner?

Emerging from the toilet, she saw him lean one elbow

against the counter while he talked with the man behind it and with the girl cleaning the inside tables. His face broke into a smile as soon as he saw her and, saying something brief to the barman, he came toward her, his gaze on hers.

There was something purposeful about his gait, catching at her breath, forcing her to wonder how his loose-limbed body would look without its clothes, striding toward her like this. She swallowed.

He stopped close in front of her, placing both hands on her waist—her naked waist, where low-slung trousers and cropped top failed to meet. His fingers seemed to burn her skin, shooting sparks of pleasure down to every nerve ending. Heat gathered in her stomach, spreading dangerously lower.

"Via," he said, his voice low and warm like a caress. "Do you want to have dinner with me? Tonight?"

She laughed, happy to discard all the careful, elaborately casual words she'd planned in the bathroom. He'd done it all so much more simply. He smiled back, his grip on her waist tightening, his thumb stroking her naked skin until it was all she could do not to gasp.

"All right," she said as calmly as she could. "If it will stop you squeezing me to death."

As she spoke, she took hold of his wrists to tug his hands off her. He let her, smiling and murmuring, "It won't."

"I suppose I'll have to take the risk." She walked back outside, glancing provocatively over her shoulder. He was smiling, but that look of lust was in his eyes again, and she could feel it burning into her nape as he followed her. She let her hips swing, remembering with some pride the way the new cotton pants hugged her rear.

He sat close to her, leaning back a little, so that when he spoke, his breath tickled her hair. She could feel the heat of his arms, his bare legs, and yet, unless she moved and brushed against him, he never touched her. It was maddening, as if he knew exactly how badly she wanted his touch again and was deliberately withholding his favors.

Turning to him, she challenged, "So, where do you want to go for dinner?"

He smiled. "How about your apartment?"

Phew—up a gear! "Cheapskate."

He shrugged. "You owe me a taxi fare."

"I owe *Lucca* a taxi fare."

"So, you two are going for dinner?" Lucca interrupted, grinning. "Can we come?"

"No," said Giancarlo, his lustful gaze never leaving Via's face. Suddenly, she was panicked again. The lightness of the afternoon had turned suddenly into some heavier flirtation she couldn't handle. It was too much for her. It thrilled her. His eyes, boring into hers, swallowing her whole, excited her beyond measure. She couldn't bear to leave his company, and yet she needed air or she'd melt into a puddle of desire at his feet, agree to things she didn't want and didn't need. Today he was not in gallant mode. He was hunting.

She said, "Supposing I meet you back here in...an hour? You choose the restaurant and we'll split the bill fifty-fifty?"

His gaze grew speculative. The girl in yellow mocked, "She's going home to change, Giancarlo. Not that you deserve it. She'll make you look like a beach bum."

Via flushed. She had, indeed, every intention of changing, but not for him. Really, not for him. She said, "I'm not used to your heat. I need to shower, put on fresh clothes."

"We'll smarten him up for you, too," said the girl in yellow, whose name was Angelina.

"Yes, well, stop short of a tuxedo," Via advised, getting to her feet. Giancarlo rose, too, helping her collect her shopping bags and walking with her as far as the pavement.

He said lightly, "I'm only flirting, you know. You don't have to leave."

She took her bags from him and, with her sunglasses firmly in place, glanced up at him, challenging. "Afraid I won't come back?"

"Yes."

Via laughed and strolled away from him. She'd walked several yards before it occurred to her that she was going the wrong way. The river was in front of her! Panicked, she whisked round. *Café on the corner, next turning away from it—got it.*

Hastily, she crossed the street, hoping nobody would notice her going back the way she had just come.

Only a little more than an hour later, she approached the café again, thinking how ironic it would be if Giancarlo was the one who didn't turn up. Freshly showered, with her thick, dark blonde hair well-washed, conditioned and brushed to a furious shine so that she was not ashamed to let it fall loose around her shoulders, she now wore a white linen dress that clung to her breasts and waist and hips, yet still swung comfortably around her knees. The straps of the dress left her shoulders and back almost naked, giving her the chance to show off the new golden-brown hue of her skin. The neckline was low enough to hint at cleavage without displaying it. Unless she leaned forward, of course.

Oh God, he's not here! At the two joined tables in the café porch, only Lucca and Angelina remained. Numbly, she walked on, wondering whether just to keep going.

"*Ciao*, Via!" shouted the yellow girl. "*Bella*," she approved, leaning her head back for a better look as Via moved toward her. "We sent Giancarlo home to change, but I don't think you'll notice much difference."

"Where is he?" Via asked casually.

Lucca jerked his head inside, so, with a faint smile, Via walked past to look for him, anxious to get this part of the evening over with. As it happened, she met him sooner than expected, in the café doorway as he came out.

Coming to an abrupt halt with their bodies almost touching, Via saw with relief that his eyes lit up with pleasure.

"Wow," he said, his voice husky with awe. He took her hands while his gaze raked her from the top of her head downward. Partly as a defense, though also just because she wanted to, Via looked, too. Still supremely casual, he now wore long, cotton trousers and a slightly more formal short-sleeved shirt, open at the throat. It didn't hide his size or his strength, and Via yearned to put her arms around that big body and press herself into him. She wanted to drown in his amazing, intense eyes, keeping her own wide open while they kissed...

As if he read her thoughts, Giancarlo suddenly pushed her hands behind her back, using the purchase that gave him to whisk her inside, behind the open café door, and pull her close against him. And God, yes, he was hard and growing harder by the instant. His cock must be huge, she thought helplessly while hot moisture pooled between her legs. What would it feel like pushing into her? What sort of a lover would he be?

And suddenly, with his mouth hovering so closely over hers that she could feel his breath on her lips, she knew without doubt or hesitancy that they would be lovers tonight, and she welcomed it with pure, uncomplicated longing.

Breathlessly, she smiled up at him, and he smiled back. Though his dark eyes were sheer lust, his hold was loose, gentle, his full lips so expressive of humor and vulnerability that they had to be kissed.

He said unsteadily, "Are you ready to eat?"

"Whenever you are," she managed.

"I'm looking forward to dessert."

Laughter caught in her throat. He smiled again and released her. "Give me one minute? I have to pay my bill."

While he went back in to pay, Via went out into the early evening sunshine and sat down beside Angelina. She felt as if she were floating on air. Very turbulent, dangerously exciting air. The knowledge that she was about to enter into something special, probably the most special relationship of her life, was both intoxicating and terrifying, but there was no room for doubt in her mind or her heart now. She wanted this, wherever it led.

"Giancarlo's a lucky man," Lucca observed, toasting her with his coffee cup. Via laughed with her usual self-disparagement. "No, seriously," Lucca pursued. "It's been so good for Giancarlo to meet you. I haven't seen him so happy, so alive, for months."

Via looked at him more seriously, vague thoughts of a broken relationship and split families reminding her that she still knew nothing about Giancarlo's personal life.

"Was he very depressed?" she asked as subtly as she could.

Lucca blinked. "Wouldn't *you* be if the doctors gave you six months to live?"

Via's ears began to sing. A huge weight dropped from nowhere onto her heart, expelling the euphoria of moments ago and replacing it with muddled disbelief and horror.

"Lucca," Angelina snapped.

"Sorry," Lucca muttered, shifting in his seat. "I thought you knew..."

"Knew what?" Via demanded, hearing the panic in her own voice as if from very far away.

"Perhaps it would come better from him," Lucca mumbled.

"You've started now, idiot," the girl said angrily, then, turning to Via she explained, "Giancarlo had cancer. A brain tumor. A year ago, the doctors gave him only six months to live. Since then, he's had a successful operation to remove the tumor and a heavy course of chemotherapy. Now it's looking better. He *seems* healthy as a horse and he's just waiting for the next all-clear from the doctors."

The words battered against her, demanding to be understood. Via grasped the table top, hard, just as Giancarlo came out, calling something back over his shoulder to someone inside, still grinning as his restless gaze sought and found her.

His step faltered. Slowly, the smiled faded from his lips, and Via saw that it was over.

Chapter Four

Giancarlo could tell at once that she knew. The wide, beautiful green eyes that had stared into his only minutes ago, so deliciously full of desire and infectious excitement, now held panic, pity, fear and grief.

It was over.

His chance of tonight with the sweet and beautiful girl who'd troubled his thoughts and dreams all week, was spoiled. Bloody Lucca with his big, stupid mouth had told her, had contaminated their spontaneous attraction with the ugliest emotion of them all: compassion. Disappointment raged through him, and not just because he'd go another night without sexual release in a woman's arms, *this* woman's arms, but because he'd lost her smile and her happiness, the vital, earthy tug of her passion. He'd read it in her face moments ago, but he wouldn't see it again.

Almost, Giancarlo turned back into the café, to lock himself in the toilet like a love-crossed adolescent. But over the last year, especially, he'd grown used to hiding his feelings. Often it helped to replace them with others. And so he kept moving, sure she would have seen nothing untoward in his expression.

"Ready?" he asked, and Via stood obediently, just as if she wouldn't, like him, rather be in any other place in the world right now. Well, they both just had to get through the evening for the sake of their own separate prides, and then they would never see each other again. Thank God.

"*Ciao*, Angelina," he said, leaving Lucca out of his farewell and callously ignoring the younger man's hurt as he and Via walked out onto the pavement.

Distress radiated from her like a beacon, irritating him beyond endurance. Fortunately, it was silent distress, he thought savagely as they moved along the road toward the bridge. If she'd been one of those women who insisted on talking about everything, he'd have gone insane.

"Giancarlo!"

With something akin to relief, they both turned to see Angelina running toward them, her yellow trousers flashing gold in the low, evening sunshine. Giancarlo walked back to meet her, while Via waited uncertainly where he'd left her.

"What?" he said. "Did I forget something?"

"Your brain, Giancarlo." Taking him by both arms, she shook him. "Don't mess this up."

"I don't know what you mean."

"I mean it's obvious to anyone with half a brain that you like her. A lot. And she can't take her eyes off you. It doesn't matter that she knows. If you push her away, you'll be sorry for the rest of your life."

"Thank you, Angelina," he said with bored patience, and saw her hand flex for a good slap. He laughed, dodging out of her way, and strode back the way he'd come, never looking directly at Via.

To cover the silence, he whistled.

Via said, "*Il Trovatore.*"

"What?" Taken by surprise, he stopped whistling to look down at her. She was gazing straight ahead.

"*Il Trovatore*," she repeated. "Verdi. It's what was playing in your car—Lucca's car—the night you found me."

"You found *me*," he contradicted. "I only stopped on command. Do you like opera?" *Have to talk about something after all.*

"I don't know. I've never been. I like some of the tunes. Lucca told me you had cancer."

Whoa, out of the blue! Interesting technique.

"I know he did," Giancarlo said gently.

Now she turned her head and looked at him. There was no accusation there, but hurt was worse. And the damnable pity. "Why didn't *you*?"

"Because I didn't want a night spent like this."

Her eyes flashed. That was good.

"*You* asked *me*, remember?"

"I did," he agreed. "But that was before you felt *obliged* to go through with it."

"*Obliged?*" She stared at him. "Why should I feel *obliged* now more than before?"

Giancarlo laughed. "Come on, Via. Don't pretend nothing's changed, that it doesn't make a difference."

"It doesn't. How shallow do you think I am?"

"Oh, no, it's not about you. It's about me. I have cancer. I might die. Of course you look at me differently. You pity me. You worry if you could cope with more than a one-night stand."

"I don't recall offering a one-night stand," she said coldly.

He lifted his eyebrows. "No? You want a full relationship? You want to live with me, nurse me, watch me die?"

Her face whitened. Cruelly, he laughed again. "No, I thought not. I must point out that death is not guaranteed at this point. However, no one voluntarily takes up with someone in my condition. It's bad enough when you have no choice, and everyone's lost *somebody* from cancer, haven't they? Even you."

"Even me," she agreed. Her voice was stony. She wasn't looking at him now. He'd achieved a good distance, he thought dispassionately. With luck she'd slap him and leave him before they even reached the restaurant.

Pushing hard now, he enquired, "Yes? Who would that have been then? Great-aunt? Neighbor? Dog?"

"My best friend and both my parents."

"Oh, Jesus Christ." He swung his arm up and around her, hugging her roughly to his side, pressing his cheek hard onto the top of her head. Her hair smelled so good, of sweet, fresh herbs and some unnamed scent he already associated with her. And he was being such a bastard.

Her body shuddered in his hold. He didn't give her time to recover from her surprise and resist him. Squeezing his eyes shut, he tried to eject the emotion once more, then he let her go and continued to stride along the road.

"Okay. I apologize for that one. Do you want to go home?"

"For hot sex?" she demanded. "Or are you withdrawing your invitation to dinner?"

The stunned laughter was out before he could prevent it. And when he looked down at her, he saw that her face was flushed. Her eyes held the sheen of suppressed moisture. Even more disarmingly, they showed no hurt or anger, just challenge as they met his with conscious bravery.

Giancarlo liked her. He couldn't help admiring her courage and her spirit. She looked like a goddess, and he wanted to wine her and dine her and take her home for the fucking of her life and his. What a bastard things weren't different. What a bastard that *he* wasn't different. He might be desperate for a lay, but he was damned if he'd make love to a woman who thought it was an act of valor just to go to dinner with him.

Well, isn't it? whispered a small voice in his head. *Haven't you made it so by being a complete jerk?*

"Hot sex," he answered. "You can choose the positions."

Another flush rose quickly up her neck to her cheeks. She looked away, pretending to examine the clothes in the shop window they were passing. "What makes you think I want to?"

"Submissive type, are you? I like that."

"I suppose you have to," she retorted.

He laughed and came to a halt. "So what's it to be? Hot sex or dinner?"

She looked him up and down. "Dinner," she said. Holding her gaze, he reached round behind her. He felt her breathing quicken.

"After you," he murmured, and wickedly enjoyed her confusion as she realized he'd merely been pushing open the restaurant door.

It was a restaurant he knew well, family run, excellent food, friendly service. He'd looked forward to bringing her here, sitting with her in the quiet window seat he'd specially asked for, learning about her, laughing with her, watching her. Well, he might still have difficulty keeping his eyes off her, particularly when she leaned forward over the menu, but now he had nothing to say and he'd never felt less like laughing in his life.

So, extracting what pleasure he could from the situation, he focused on her cleavage, admiring the swell of her breasts rising from the strapless bra that seemed to push them upward and together. He imagined easing his tongue down there as a prelude to removing the bra altogether. The beast in his underpants stirred.

"Like what you see?"

His blatant staring had brought a flush to her cheeks once more. Giancarlo sat back. "I'd like to see more."

"Tough," she said, just as the waiter came to take their order. Without waiting for him, she ordered her own food in very respectable Italian and asked for a bottle of water.

"Sure you don't want wine?" Giancarlo prompted. "I think you might need it to make the evening bearable."

"Why, are you planning on being horrible again?" she enquired, handing her menu back to the waiter.

"I don't plan it," he said, not quite truthfully. "It just happens."

She couldn't respond to that at once, because he gave the waiter his order. And when he'd finished and turned to her for her retort, she asked, "So, are you really a policeman?"

Taken by surprise by this civilized tack, he agreed that he was.

"Carabinieri?" she enquired.

"Yes," he said again.

"I should have known when the young officer came to the hotel so quickly. I suppose you work with him?"

"Not directly, but he knows who I am."

"He smirked when he called you 'Giancarlo'."

"I'm not surprised. It's the only chance he'll get to do so."

Her eyes widened. "You outrank him?"

He wondered with unexpected amusement if she was trying to rile him by sounding so astonished. Leaning back in his chair, he said, "Yes, but I'm also bigger than he is."

A girl brought a bottle of water and glasses, and Giancarlo

watched as Via poured for both of them. Her face was calm, almost tranquil, yet he thought her hands shook slightly. His conscience smote him, along with a wicked satisfaction. He knew she'd done nothing wrong, and yet some cruel part of him wanted her to suffer because his illness made a difference to her. She was fighting it, of course, trying to do the right thing, and that effort was unendurable.

"So, do you work here in Pisa?" she asked, still making the conversation for both of them. She set the bottle down. "When you're not on leave?"

He shrugged. "Often. I have an apartment here. My unit's based in Rome, but I move around a lot."

"What unit is that?"

"Special Operations. Organized crime, fraud, drugs. The seamy side of life."

"Do you like it?"

"*Like* it?" His lips twisted into something approaching a smile. "No, I don't suppose I like it. But it's important to me."

She'd been playing with her glass, gazing into it rather than at him, but at that her fingers stilled. "Yes? That sounded almost sincere."

He let out a hiss of laughter. "I am sincere. What's the matter, Via? Hasn't your work ever been important to you?"

"What, the bottling factory? Hardly."

"Some other job, then."

"No." She didn't even think about it. "They were all tedious. With the exception of my fortnight in Pisa, and look where that got me."

"Dinner with me. Bad luck. Why don't you get a different kind of job?"

She shrugged. "It's difficult. I've got no qualifications."

"Go to university."

She looked at him as if he had horns. "They wouldn't have me. I've never passed an exam in my life. Apart from my B in Standard Grade Art."

He stirred, interested in spite of himself. "How come?"

She shrugged. "I'm slow at reading and writing. So I used to lose interest and misbehave instead. Why don't *you* go to university?"

Ignoring that, he said, "Are you dyslexic?"

That got her attention. "So they say. How did you guess?"

"Slow reading? Via being easier than Victoria to write? Your shocking sense of direction, and the notes and arrows scrawled all over your map?"

She flushed, looking so pointlessly, adorably defiant that he found himself saying, "There's no shame in dyslexia, you know. It shouldn't be a barrier to your education, either."

"Yes, well, I wasn't diagnosed until the year I left school. I was the one who slipped through the net, even though it's not meant to happen now. It doesn't matter. I'm fine as I am."

He smiled. "I think so," he said warmly, before he remembered. As if embarrassed, she took a large gulp of water, and this time it was he who looked away. With relief, he saw their pasta arriving.

It could have been worse, he thought as they walked back over the bridge toward her apartment. Dinner had had its awkward moments, but at times he'd forgotten everything but her company and, in spite of himself, he still enjoyed that. He even liked just looking at her, even when it tortured him unbearably to do so.

Via paused, looking up the broad, curving sweep of the

river. It was dark now, and the moonlight reflected in the Arno's gently rippling water. It made a pretty, romantic picture, the girl in white gazing out from the bridge at the rows of imposing buildings on either bank. It would have been pleasant to stand beside her, his arm around her bare shoulders, perhaps turn her to him for a long, sweet kiss.

Giancarlo's lips twisted as he sneered at himself. He was long past the stage of such romantic boy-meets-girl nonsense. And this night was about to end. Not the ending he'd hoped for when he first saw her walking along the road toward the café, but hell, what had he lost out of it?

Just take the girl home and leave her. She'll be as glad as you to say good night. After all, she's been carrying the conversation for the last two hours. She thinks you're a boring jerk, and she's right.

As if she heard him, she turned from the river view and walked on. As he fell into silent step beside her, he felt her warm, smooth fingers brush the skin of his hand, shooting little arrows of awareness through his already too-sensitive body. To his amazement, her fingers turned, taking hold of his, sliding into his palm.

Christ, she was holding hands. She was still trying to salvage the evening. But she wasn't looking at him. Her skin deliciously flushed, she gazed ahead, turning occasionally to the river, waiting for him to make some response to her overture. Her profile was beautiful; her delicate bone structure looked as if it would snap under the strength of his caresses. As he watched, still stunned by her perseverance, he saw her lips part, her tongue slip out to wet them nervously. She drew her lower lip between her teeth, and desire growled through Giancarlo's body.

Leaving the bridge, he realized that despite his best efforts to put her off, she was still prepared to sleep with him. Compassion, he thought savagely, was a truly astonishing force. Well, he wouldn't do that to her, but, by God, he'd wipe the pity out of her eyes before he left her.

He said, "Do you know how much I've wanted to kiss you?" She stumbled. Her grip tightened as she regained her balance, and he added softly, "All over?"

Her laughter was a little breathless. Under his finger on her wrist, her pulse raced, and he knew he still affected her. He felt exultant. If he got any harder, he wouldn't be able to walk. But he made no effort to hide his erection, and when he saw her gaze flicker down to it and linger, he was fiercely glad.

"So, where is this apartment of yours?" he asked as they passed the café.

"Next turning," she said, and coughed a little as if to hide the trembling of her voice. Was she scared of him or—surely not now—just as desperate as he was to make love?

"Are you going to invite me in?" he asked.

She smiled nervously. "For coffee?" she teased.

"I was thinking of the hot sex again, but coffee's a start."

She laughed, and he caressed the soft skin between her thumb and forefinger. At the side of the bakery, she led him through a gate and up a rickety flight of steps to a tiny garden. There, while he gazed over the darkened roofs, she unlocked the French doors.

"Quick," she said, "before the mosquitoes get in."

He brushed past her into the house. She snapped the light on, saying, "Coffee, then?"

"Stuff the coffee," said Giancarlo roughly, reaching for her with both hands. Her shoulders were soft and warm under his fingers, setting the blood pounding afresh in his tortured body.

Her green eyes looked huge as they gazed up into his, betraying hope as well as anxiety and, when he slid his fingers under the straps of her dress, a desire surely as fierce as his own. "I want my kiss," he whispered, easing the straps away so they fell down her arms. With one finger, he traced the neckline of her dress as it dropped lower across her breasts, stroking as far as the bra would let him.

Her skin was flushed, her breathing too quick and unsteady. He bent his head, noticing with fierce triumph that her lips parted for him, as if of their own volition. A moment longer, he let his lips hover there, increasing the anticipation. Then, closing his palm over her breast, he took her mouth in his.

A sigh that was almost a moan broke from her. She opened for him at once, sweetly responsive. She tasted of coffee and tiramisu and something simply Via, and he couldn't get enough of her. He caught her tongue around his, twisting, dancing, drawing it into his own mouth. As he deepened the kiss, she moaned again, pushing her body into him so hard that he stumbled back against the door. Her lips and teeth were suddenly wild, sucking and biting him to insanity while her body writhed against him.

Without breaking the astounding kiss, he grasped her by the waist, lifting her, turning her so he could hold her captive against the door and grind his hardness into her. At the same time, he pushed down her bra, seeking and finding her pebbled nipples, stroking over and over with his thumb, then pinching until she all but sobbed. Her hands were on his back, burrowing under his shirt, running all over his naked skin until he wondered if he was actually capable of drawing back now.

As if she heard his desperate thought, she gasped against his lips. "You said if you kissed me, you wouldn't stop."

"That was last week," he said, and dived back into her mouth. He roved his hands over her hips, down her thighs, feeling with ferocious joy every tiny movement of her responsive flesh. His fingers caught the hem of her dress and tugged.

Tearing his lips free of hers for a moment, he whispered, "Do you know what I want to do?"

Laughter trembled on her swollen lips. "I could hazard a guess!"

He reached between her legs, making her gasp again. She was so hot, the wispy cotton covering her so wet, that he groaned with the genuine anguish of utter loss. But he wouldn't stop, not yet.

"I want to push my cock right inside you now, fuck you 'til you beg for mercy. Would you like that, Via? Would you?"

Her fingers grasped his arms. She pushed against the hand on her pussy, twisting. "Stop talking, Giancarlo," she said shakily. "Just do it!"

He buried his face in her hair so that his voice came out low and muffled. "That's the bastard, Via. I won't."

She grew very still. Through the silence, he could hear only her wild, erratic breathing. Slowly, deliberately, he removed his hand from between her legs, then, taking her own fingers from their strong grip on his arm, he carried them to her pussy.

He lifted his head until he could see her wild eyes, clouded with desire and incomprehension. "Use your fingers," he whispered. "In the long run, it will be better for us both."

He kissed her bemused mouth once more and let her go. "Besides, it will give me something to fantasize about in the long walk home. *Arrivederci.*"

He couldn't look at her stunned face as he moved her aside and opened the door. He couldn't bear to see her hurt.

He couldn't bear himself.

Though he wasn't asleep, it took three rings of the bell before he troubled to answer the door. And even then he did so only because Angelina was yelling through the letterbox. "Giancarlo, I know you're in there!"

Dressed for work at eight o'clock in the morning, she was blindingly smart and vital. Her no-nonsense eyes scanned his briefly at the door. Then she said, "You messed it up."

Giancarlo walked back into his living room, leaving the front door open. He knew she would follow him, and she did, demanding, "What happened?"

He threw himself onto the sofa and shrugged. "Nothing. Do you want coffee?"

"No."

There was silence while she stood in front of him, waiting. At last, reluctantly, he began to speak.

"She was trying hard, so hard I knew it couldn't come from the heart. But I couldn't leave it. I couldn't bear for the last expression I saw in her eyes to be pity. So I changed that look and left her."

Frowning, Angelina sank beside him. "You came on to her until she wanted you and then left her?"

An unhappy smile tugged at the corner of his lips at this succinct summary of events. "Something like that. And do you know what's worst of all?"

"That you were a total bastard?"

"No. Though of course I was. That I think now maybe it did come from the heart. Even the trying."

"Oh, Giancarlo, you idiot. Were you really so awful? Is it beyond repair?"

"Yes and yes. Definitely."

Angelina opened her mouth again, but to his relief, the doorbell rang before she could say anymore. When Giancarlo made no move, Angelina rose and went to answer it. Waiting for her to see off this unwelcome visitor, he stared out at nothing, going over last night's events in his head yet again and trying in vain to find any excuse for his conduct.

By the time it penetrated that Angelina had not only failed to get rid of the visitor but had invited him in, the man was in his living room. Blinking, Giancarlo took in the uniform of the Carabinieri.

Chapter Five

For the first time that week, Via was still at home beyond noon. She felt curiously numb, if it was possible to be numb and furious at the same time. Disappointment was far sharper than it should have been, considering the length of her acquaintance with him, but she'd expected more of the man who had saved her life and shown her such kindness that night, in his quiet, understated way.

But God, there'd been nothing understated about him last night! He had deliberately humiliated her to satisfy his own perverse pride, and there was no excuse for that, not even illness.

Leaving the French doors open, she took her Italian phrase book and a bowl of fresh olives out onto the tiny roof garden and tried to distract herself. Of course, she'd made too much of meeting him again. The dependency she'd felt on their first meeting just hadn't properly worn off. She'd probably seemed an easy lay, just another British tourist "gagging for it".

But no, this was *not* her fault, and she was damned if she'd take the blame. It hadn't been like that until Lucca had told her about his cancer. Before that he'd definitely liked her, and although he'd no doubt been thinking about it rather more casually than she, that didn't bother her. Every relationship had to begin somewhere. But he had *liked* her, not just wanted into her knickers, she could swear it. Only then he'd turned into a dangerously petulant kid and spoiled everything, including the fun of her holiday.

She wished she'd never spotted him in the café yesterday, never approached him there. Before that moment, she'd been happy with her lot, extracting everything she could from her time here. Now it felt spoiled, churned up. And she hated the man who'd been her hero. Ridiculously, it felt a lot like grief.

Sighing, Via leaned back against the sweet-scented lemon tree, gazing over the roofs to the distant mountains. Perhaps she should leave Pisa, go up into the hills? Or to the coast? Only she'd paid for this flat and she couldn't really afford anywhere else now. And it was pleasant here, in her tiny garden. Her eyes closed against the hazy blue sky, letting only the sounds of the town filter into her consciousness—the noise of ubiquitous Italian traffic all over the city, a dog barking in the street below, a bicycle bell. Two men calling to each other in good-natured banter, children laughing, their feet pounding the pavement below as they played.

She could smell new bread from the bakery, and some herby, tomato and onion concoction that made her mouth water. Closer to home, the delightful scent of the lemon tree mingled with the mix of flowers, soothing her.

Below, a gate creaked. She heard footsteps and realized with a jolt that it had been *her* gate, that someone was coming up the steps to her garden.

Giancarlo, was her first immediate thought and, in spite of everything, her heart jolted at the possibility. Because she wanted the opportunity to tell him off, she insisted. And she wouldn't accept any apology he might be here to make.

While her heart thudded, she deliberately kept her eyes closed until the footsteps reached the top. Only then did she turn her head, gazing into the dazzling sun. She had to shield her eyes before she could make out the uniform of the Carabinieri.

Surprise had her stumbling to her feet. The phrase book tumbled from her lap into the grass before she even recognized the English-speaking policeman who had interviewed her at the Hotel Leonardo. Then it registered that he wasn't alone, that behind the smartly turned out young man came the bald head and supremely casual figure of Giancarlo in shorts and T-shirt.

"*Buona sera, signorina.*"

"*Buona sera.*" She didn't look at Giancarlo. "How can I help you?"

"Well, we have some more information about your case," the young man said in English, although she had addressed him in Italian. "And some more questions, if you don't mind."

"I see." Her gaze flickered to Giancarlo, who chose to lounge against the garden fence, watching her. She had the impression his face was deliberately expressionless, but she didn't let her gaze linger, instead turning it on the younger man. "Do you want to come inside?"

"We can sit out here if you're comfortable."

Shrugging, Via sat back down against the tree. While the policeman perched on the edge of the one garden chair, Giancarlo eased himself off the fence and strolled the few steps toward them. *Bastard!* Even from the corner of her eye, the movement of his big body inside his loose clothes set her nerves tingling. Via pushed the bowl of olives toward the younger man. She didn't dare lift it to offer it more politely, in case Giancarlo saw her hands shaking.

With a quick glance at Giancarlo, who squatted on the ground and reached easily for an olive, the policeman said, "We think we have found the place where you were...assaulted."

"I'm sorry, I'm rotten at directions," Via apologized.

"It wasn't difficult from your description," he assured her, "and with the help of the captain, it took no time at all."

She frowned. It was on the tip of her tongue to enquire who the captain was, when the truth came to her. She couldn't prevent her quick glance of surprise, for she knew a captain of the Carabinieri was a high-ranking officer. Giancarlo's eyebrows shot up. It was a comical gesture of self-mockery: *see how important I am?* And once it would have made her laugh and like him for it. Only she'd discovered he wasn't really that person at all.

"We're still collecting evidence. From the site and from your robe, we should be able to collect enough DNA to convict most of the youths concerned."

Via nodded. The policeman cast another glance at Giancarlo. "Unfortunately, we also discovered a body."

Via's stomach twisted. She felt the blood drain from her face, leaving her dizzy. "Jesus," she whispered. "Who?"

"A girl who went missing last year. She had been murdered, beaten and stabbed to death. I think you had a luckier escape than you knew."

She raised her hand in a quick, troubled gesture, pushing the hair back from her face although there was no need. She didn't care now about the trembling. "No," she said, low. "I always knew they meant to kill me. Stupidly, it just never struck me that they'd done it before."

"Well, if the evidence points to the same perpetrators, and I suspect it largely does, it makes the charges against them rather more serious. The Marinuzzi twins have already been charged with your abduction and assault. Likewise, several of their friends and associates. However, all of them deny that Marinuzzi Senior was involved."

Via glared at him. “He was.”

“We have no reason to doubt that,” he assured her. “Everything else you told us has turned out to be quite true. Evidence is the problem here. We may yet get what we need from the forensics people, but so far there is nothing.” He drew in his breath, glancing again at Giancarlo. “For the moment, we have nothing to hold him on, and he has retreated with his family to his summer home in the Cinque Terre. We are hoping that from there, he will give us evidence.”

“How? By trying to throw it in the sea?” Via seized an olive and hurled it so hard it splatted against the French door. How bloody typical that the prime mover, the controller, was the one who got away.

Giancarlo stirred. He said, “No—by coming after you.”

Via stared at him. “What?”

“Did you never ask yourself why they picked you? Why deliberately attract someone from a foreign country, lull her into a false sense of security for two weeks, then try and sacrifice her to the Devil? Why not just grab a passing vagrant?”

She snorted. “Perhaps they thought I was a virgin.”

“Perhaps they thought you were something even more significant. Via, how many brothers do you have?”

She blinked. “Six, for my sins.”

“All older?”

“Yes, but…”

“Then you are a seventh child? And how many siblings did your mother have?”

Via licked her lips. “All right. Now you’re being too weird. So I’m the seventh child of a seventh child. That’s rare in this day and age, but I still don’t see how it benefits them to kill me.”

"To *sacrifice* you. The gift of your life would be all the greater because of *your* gifts."

"*What* gifts?" Via demanded with hostility.

"Don't you have any?" asked the policeman hopefully. "ESP of any kind?"

"No."

Giancarlo took another olive. He said, "When you first told me what happened, you said it was almost familiar, as if you'd been there before. Do you have second sight, Via?"

She shook her head. "Of course not," she said shakily. "Second sight is an old wives' tale, like the seventh child nonsense."

"Undoubtedly. But I think maybe you see *unusual* things, in dreams maybe, which you talked about as a child if at no other time. I think you or your family told your Italian neighbor, who let it drop to his friend Marinuzzi, and I think that is why you were... chosen."

"Well, *I* think *you* are havering!"

"Havering?" repeated the policeman, frowning with incomprehension. He seemed to be affronted that he didn't know the word.

"It's Scots," Via said with satisfaction, "and it means talking rubbish. Like your *captain*."

"I'm not *his* captain," Giancarlo said, unruffled. "It might be rubbish to you and me and the rest of the unmurderous population. But to Marinuzzi, I think it meant something. Some power the sacrifice of you at the right time would give him. The murdered girl's family said she was telepathic. Which is why I don't think he'd pass up the chance of another go at you."

"Then thank God I'm in Pisa and he's in the Cinque Terre. Wherever that is."

Again she saw the younger man glance at Giancarlo, who appeared merely bland as he bit the last olive flesh off a stone.

The young policeman said, "The captain's family live near the Cinque Terre."

Oh no. Not on your life!

"How nice for the captain. Then he'll have somewhere to stay when he goes up there to arrest the bastard."

"I'm on leave," said Giancarlo.

"Which means the Carabineri would not officially be involved. Marinuzzi could not accuse us of harassment. But if you went up with him, as his guest..."

Giancarlo smiled into the distance.

"Marinuzzi might well try to kidnap you again."

"Oh, good," Via said with savage sarcasm.

"But you will be perfectly safe," the young man assured her, "because you will be protected by the captain."

"Oh, yes, safe as houses."

He looked perplexed. Unable to sit still any longer, Via sprang to her feet, striding round the tiny garden.

"You go back to work, Manfredi," Giancarlo murmured. "Via will make up her own mind. I'll keep you informed."

Manfredi stood, with apparent relief, bowing to Via and nodding to Giancarlo. For a moment he looked as if he was about to salute, but Giancarlo forestalled him, eyes glinting. "Well done," he observed with a grin, and the young man could only flash a smile of response before he fled.

Via strode on, though the garden was so small she began to feel dizzy. She was also very aware of Giancarlo's gaze following her. At last, stopping dead, she stared fixedly at the mountain.

"How old was she?"

Giancarlo didn't pretend to misunderstand. "Seventeen."

"Christ." Abruptly she turned to face him. "What is it you want me to do?"

"Come home with me. We'll get the word around. I'll do a little snooping. I'm fairly sure there's a bit of Satanism going on round there with or without him. And I'll make damn sure he doesn't actually reach you. An attempt is all we need."

With an effort, Via evened her breathing. At last, she walked slowly toward him and sat back down in her old place under the tree. This time, with pride in her own courage, she looked directly into his face.

"All right, before I agree to anything, we had better understand each other. You saved my life last week, and for that I will always be grateful. But I don't like you, Giancarlo. You're not the man I thought you were. And if I do this, it's not for you—it's for the girl who did die, and for any who might if we don't try."

He didn't flinch. He didn't even look angry. When she'd finished, he only nodded once in acceptance. "Fair enough."

Oh Jesus, what am I doing? Am I more afraid of him or Marinuzzi?

"Then I'll do it."

His lips quirked upward. "Good girl." He rose fluidly to his feet. "I'll pick you up tomorrow morning at eight. *Ciao.*"

When he could no longer see her, her lips twisted in return. "*Ciao*, Giancarlo," she said to his disappearing back.

It wasn't easy, sitting beside him on the long drive up the Tuscan coast. The best of the views were always out of his window, and she had to gaze past his distinctive profile to get to them. She was reminded too forcefully of her first drive in his company, when she'd found him fearsome at the beginning, then unnecessarily kind. And now—now she knew he was unnecessarily *un*kind, and yet something about him still moved her, still inspired her with lust and other less specific longings. She didn't know what she thought of him anymore.

At least watching the view was a reason to look in his direction, an excuse to study him. He was, she knew, a man of strong personality. It shone out of his clear, intelligent face and his almost frighteningly bright, intense eyes. Yet the odd delicacy she'd first observed in her hotel room seemed now to be vulnerability, and not just to illness. She quite understood his desire for a fling with someone totally free from the taint of awareness of his cancer. And she was dangerously close to forgiving him his unforgivable reaction.

Since his gaze was on the road in front, she allowed her own to stray downward over his bulging biceps to his bronzed, muscled thighs and calves, back up to the big hands resting lightly on the steering wheel, and the tattoos snaking up from his wrists. The man's body had stayed fit, she thought suddenly, or recovered fitness. It was his mind, his spirit, that was damaged.

Her throat closed up. She glanced away just as his head turned toward her. "What?"

"Nothing," she muttered, erasing all softer emotion from her face before she allowed herself to meet his gaze. "I just wish you'd keep your attention on the road," she snapped.

"It *is* on the road," he objected, sparing it a quick glance.

"At a ninety degree angle?" she enquired, and his face creased into a grin as he turned to the windscreen once more.

"I have an eye in the side of my head."

"Yes, well it's a pity then that your head is generally so far up your..."

"Signorina," he interrupted with mock shock. "You sound just like my wife!"

In spite of everything, an unpleasant jolt twisted through her stomach.

"Which is fortunate," he continued, "if you're going to pretend to be my girlfriend."

"Am I?" she said, startled enough to be briefly distracted.

"It's the only viable cover for you to be with me."

"Won't your wife mind?" she asked, sarcastically polite.

He smiled faintly, keeping his eyes on the road. "No, she's an ex-wife."

"Sorry," she murmured. Then, as casually as she could, "For long?"

"Long married? No. Long divorced? Ten years."

"Do you have children?" she asked. How little she knew of him, and how much she had made out of nothing.

"God, no," he said, grinning again. "Angelina is not maternal. Or not yet she isn't."

"Angelina?" she repeated, startled.

"You met her."

"The girl in yellow?"

"That's her."

Via swallowed that. It took a little time. Then she said, "She seems very fond of you."

"We've been friends a long time."

"I see."

He turned his attention from the road again to laugh at her. "No, you don't."

"Truck," yelled Via.

"I see it. It's on the other side of the road."

At least on *the road. Unlike your eyes!*

"Angelina's in love with Lucca. Idiot drunk as he is."

She looked at him quizzically. "Do you mind?"

He shrugged. "I'll be happier when he's grown up. No, I don't mind. What I minded was being married to her."

"Yes, well, I doubt you had the worst of that deal."

"True."

"Stop doing that."

"Doing what?"

"Agreeing with me." She smiled reluctantly. "It makes it very hard to quarrel with you."

"I know."

After that, although she hadn't meant to allow herself to relax with him, or even to speak to him more than was strictly necessary, it was easier.

Chapter Six

Giancarlo's family lived in a small town on the Tuscan coast. The community spread itself around the dramatic curve of a stunningly beautiful clear blue bay and strayed up the hillside behind.

"You like my town?" Giancarlo enquired, turning up a side road that led up the hill.

"The beach is horrible." Via shuddered at the sight they'd just left of hundreds of people packed on to the rocky, stony beach in row upon row of sun-loungers and umbrellas.

"In July," Giancarlo agreed. Something, a note that was almost disappointment or even hurt in his tone, made her glance at him, but for once his attention was on the road, and his face looked perfectly calm.

"The town is pretty, though, and the view is spectacular."

"It's even better from up here."

He turned off up another, even quieter street, lined by brightly painted villas in many shapes and sizes. The hill grew steeper until she began to feel the car couldn't make it.

It did, however. Blasting the horn, Giancarlo pulled into the roadside by a blue house with a round tower on one side. For a moment it seemed such an incongruous place for him to live that she asked, "Did your parents retire here?"

"No. I was born here." He switched the engine off, then for an instant paused with his fingers still gripping the keys. Expecting some sort of unwelcome comment or request, Via glanced at him. Oddly enough, she had the impression he was gathering his strength. Certainly, she heard him draw in a deep breath. Then, with a quick smile at her, he said, "All right—let's go in and get the introductions over with. Forgive them in advance, by the way. My mother's been trying to marry me off ever since Angelina left."

Since he got out of the car as he spoke, she had no opportunity to respond. By the time she had climbed out, too, there were two children and a dog running across the garden and throwing themselves at the gate, and behind them a plump woman in an apron. Following in a more leisurely manner was a tall young man with slicked back black hair and a grin.

While Giancarlo called the inevitable "*ciaos*" and casually opened the boot of the car to retrieve their two small bags, the woman loudly shooed the kids and the dog away from the gate so that she could wrench it open, and they all spilled onto the street. Giancarlo was seized in a hug tight enough to have constricted the breathing of a much healthier man and soundly kissed while the children hung onto his legs, and the dog danced round him, barking excitedly.

It would have been funny, Via thought with a sudden lump in her own throat, had it not been for the tears in the woman's eyes.

How do you deal with the knowledge that your child might die? How can you let him leave when you know he might be dead before you can see him again?

And how do you face a homecoming so fraught with these emotions that you can't forget your illness for a moment?

Via saw his mother's fear and joy, her premature grief,

understood it all absolutely, and hated it for his sake. Smiling and patient, he hugged her back, saying easily, "*Bene, bene,*" to whatever muffled questions she was all but sobbing into his chest. But Via could feel his tension as if it were her own, his relief as he finally felt able to put her gently aside so that he could joke with the children, ruffling their hair before reaching over their heads to grasp hands with the young man behind. That was easier, but even with him, the younger man scanned him anxiously, looking for any faintest sign of illness or degeneration. It was inevitable, a symptom of love, but one he clearly found hard to bear.

After only an instant, he swung free of them with a kind of massive relief, throwing one arm instead around Via, who had been standing silently behind.

"This is Via, from Scotland," he said cheerfully. "Via, my mother Antonia, my brother Mario and my sister's children, Chiara and Carlo."

Via, overwhelmed with memory induced by his sudden nearness, the solid weight of his arm on her shoulders, could only smile weakly at their warm welcome. Yet when he released her, she felt stupidly cold and alone. Trying to hide it, she turned to take her bag from him.

Without looking at her, he said, "I've got it. On you go."

This was stupid, she thought as she walked through the gate with Giancarlo's brother. He didn't want to be treated differently just because of his illness, yet here he was, forcing her to treat him differently. She wouldn't have allowed anyone else to carry her own bag.

"So, how long have you known Giancarlo?" Mario asked, walking across the gravel drive beside her.

"Oh. About a week, I suppose."

He looked slightly disappointed at that, though his mother

bustled forward to ask warmly how long she was staying in Italy.

"I'm not sure," Via said. "Another week, maybe two if the money holds out..." She tried a tentative smile, but she seemed to have disappointed the *signora*, too.

"Oh. You don't work here then?"

"No."

"The world is a small place these days, Mama," Mario consoled her. "Flights from Pisa..."

"Warned you," Giancarlo said in her ear, walking past them toward the front door.

Stupidly, it was only when his mother said, "Giancarlo, show Via to your room," that she realized the awkwardness of her situation. It had never entered her head that she might be expected to share a room—a bed!—with Giancarlo, and Antonia's words hit her like a hammer blow. Panic rose as she blindly followed him up a rather gracious staircase into an upstairs hall and along to the end, through another door and up a narrower half-flight and into a round room with windows overlooking the sea.

The sight of the astonishing room closed her mouth. White walls with old pictures of football teams and racing cars. A bookcase half-full of novels and what looked like dull text books. A teenager's room. Giancarlo hadn't really lived here for a long time. And under the window with its breathtaking view—a single bed. Giancarlo laid both their bags on it. To Via, the gesture looked symbolic.

No possibility of separation. Intolerable.

"Giancarlo, you have to tell your mother I can't sleep here."

His eyebrows rose, yet she had the feeling from the faint quirk of his lips that he understood perfectly.

"Why not? Don't you like it?"

"It's a lovely room," she said impatiently.

"I can take the Ferraris off the wall."

"Giancarlo, don't be obtuse. I will not sleep with you."

"Well, don't tell the whole household. They all think you at least want to."

"Why can't you tell them the truth? They're your family!"

"It's more convenient," he said. "My mother won't try to fix me up with her neighbors' daughters if she thinks you're my girlfriend."

"Well, I'm a very puritanical girlfriend who refuses to share a room with you, let alone a bed that size."

As his gaze followed hers to the couch in question, she realized she'd made a mistake bringing the bed into the argument. She saw a certain speculation enter his expression and knew he was imagining their naked bodies together in that tiny space. Even more annoyingly, her own imagination swept into overdrive, providing her with a brief, overwhelming vision of herself lying under him, his big, sensitive hands on her bare, heated skin, caressing her nipples, her thighs, his intense eyes blazing from his passionate face as he pushed into her over and over...

Oh, God, perhaps it wouldn't be so very bad?

Giancarlo sighed. "Well, it's a pity," he observed, "but in fact, no one has invited you to share a bed with me. I have to sleep with Mario, which is an even greater pity since he snores."

"So do I," Via said at once, whirling away to cover her indignation at the way he had led her on.

"Don't try to console me," he said wryly, picking up his own bag from the bed and walking toward the door. "There's a bathroom under the spiral stair. Come downstairs whenever you're ready." Glancing over his shoulder, he added, "You won't get lost. Just follow the noise."

Half an hour later, showered and changed into one of the new, loose linen dresses acquired in Pisa, she made her way back downstairs to the accompaniment of mouth-watering cooking aromas. Though Giancarlo had said to follow the noise, she couldn't actually hear any. She could have followed her nose, but somehow she didn't feel quite comfortable enough with these strangers to go forcing her way into their kitchen. Instead, she wandered into what looked to be a sitting room. Since nobody was in there, she'd already turned to leave again when the photographs caught her eye.

They were all over the place, on side tables, on the piano, on the mantelpiece, hanging on the walls, all of people, his family. The one that caught her eye was of Giancarlo. Staring out at her from the piano with a look of quizzical amusement in his deep, dark brown eyes, he wore the uniform and cap of the Carabinieri. Going closer, Via saw that he was younger. The laughter lines at his eyes were less pronounced, the whole set of his face somehow less hard. It must have been the day he graduated—or whatever one did—as a Carabinieri officer.

Beneath the cap, his hair was cut militarily short, but she could see it was as black as his brows. Other pictures of him were less easy to spot. In among ancient-looking wedding photographs of brides and grooms, of christenings and family groups, she finally found one of Angelina in a white dress. And beside her, looking lean and hungry and rebellious, was a ridiculously young and lanky Giancarlo. It must have been their wedding day. Angelina looked deliriously happy, leaning into him. He was laughing into the camera as if joking with whoever took the picture. He looked so different with a shock of black curls falling around his face and neck that it took Via some time to recognize him. It was the amazing eyes that gave him away.

Moving across to the next photos hanging on the wall, she spotted the long-haired Giancarlo again, this time in the academic gown and mortar board of a university graduate. He looked quizzical again here, only a faint, rather enigmatic smile playing about his lips, as if he was wondering what all the fuss was about.

From the doorway, his voice said, "Recognize him?"

Via jumped. However, stopping herself in time from turning, she said only, "I once suggested you go to university. I should have known you'd already done it."

"To be a Carabinieri officer, you need a degree in law. Don't be too overawed. They give them out like toilet paper."

"Liar," said another voice behind him, a woman's voice. "Where's the gorgeous girlfriend, then?"

Before he could move aside, a very short, very heavily pregnant woman pushed past him into the room, her gaze openly seeking and finding Via. She grinned. "There you are. I'm Lisa."

"My sister," Giancarlo said. "The kids you met on the way in belong to her."

"Ah—if you met them, you must wonder why I'm doing this again," said Lisa, pausing in her majestic sail across the room to pat her prominent bump.

"We all know why you're doing it again," Giancarlo said. "You forgot to take your pills. Again."

"Swine," said Lisa without heat. "We all know you dote on my kids. Don't you think he'd make a wonderful father, Via?"

"Maybe, when he grows up."

Lisa laughed, shooting her an appraising glance that belied her slightly ditzy appearance and manner.

Giancarlo said, “When you two have finished assassinating my character, would you like a glass of wine? We’re eating in the garden, Via, if that’s all right with you.”

Despite its beautiful setting on a terrace overlooking the sea on one side and vine-covered hills on two others, Via found dinner a little overwhelming. Giancarlo’s family were all strong personalities, from his jovial father down to Lisa’s children, and Via found herself alternately bombarded by friendly questions and bewildered by the flying conversation and swift squabbles even more swiftly made up.

Once, Mario said, “Did you study Italian at school, Via?”

“No, I’m afraid I studied very little at school.” By this time she’d discovered that not only Giancarlo but his father, his brother, sister and brother-in-law were all university graduates, and she was feeling very keenly her own lack of academic achievement. Her only defense was to laugh it off, and her comment did raise a chuckle round the table.

“How come your Italian’s so good, then?” Mario demanded.

“Is it?” Via asked, half-amused, half-startled and wholly unbelieving of this flattery. Both he and Lisa looked at her so meaningfully that she demanded, “What?”

“Yes,” Giancarlo stated beside her, “it is.”

She felt herself blushing under his unexpected praise. His bare arm brushed against hers as he reached for his glass. “I’d say you have a definite talent for languages,” he added, glancing round at her to lift the glass in a silent toast. “Worth looking into.”

Stupidly, a little glow of warmth began to spread around her heart at that. Not just because it was an idea she would indeed investigate further, but because, despite his nastiness the other night, he remembered what she’d said and was trying to help. Hell, his praise alone was music to her ears. How pathetic was that?

"Via is between jobs," he explained to his enquiring family.

"Bad luck," Lisa sympathized. "What did you do before?"

It was the question she dreaded in this company. Her heart sank, but, although part of her wanted Giancarlo to leap in and save her the embarrassment, there was a thrawn, defiant part that refused to give in to it, to be ashamed of a perfectly respectable if extremely dull job.

She reached for her own wine. "I worked in a whisky bottling factory."

"Whisky?" said Giancarlo's father. "I love whisky. That's a job you should have hung on to."

Everyone was laughing and remonstrating, and the moment passed. Dazed, Via met Giancarlo's knowing glance. The skin around his eyes crinkled in the smile that set her heart jumping, no matter how sternly she forbade it.

"So," he suggested, "I thought we could go down to the village later. Show you my favorite sights."

"His favorite bar," Mario translated. "Can we come, too?"

"No," said Lisa emphatically. "They want to be alone."

"No, we don't," Via denied.

Antonia laughed, making Via blush by observing, "Ah, she protests too much, bless her."

"Oh, I don't know," Giancarlo said lazily. "If we wanted to be alone we wouldn't go to a bar, would we? We can all go."

Lisa objected, "Anzio is always busy in the summer. Besides, the kids have taken it over this year. You'd be better going somewhere else."

"Are you saying we're too old for Anzio's?" Mario demanded. "Okay, now we *have* to go there."

In the end, only Mario and Lisa's husband Fabio accompanied them. Lisa was feeling tired, as one might expect given her condition, and the old couple insisted on washing up while the others went out.

By mutual consent, they walked down the steep hill into the village. The wine and the warmth of Giancarlo's family had soothed Via's nerves, so she found herself relaxing in the cool, evening sun, letting Italy wash over her afresh. The scents of sea salt and lemon played around the edges of her senses while the stunning sea views took her breath away. It *was* the view, she told herself severely, and nothing to do with the fact that as they approached the busier part of the town, Giancarlo casually took her hand. Playing his part, just playing his part. She would not be caught that way again, no matter how warm and good his rough fingers felt around hers.

And yet, when he dropped them just as casually to open the café door, she felt the loss with stupid, maddening strength. What *was* it about him?

Giancarlo's favorite café was on the sea front. Leaving the tourists outside, they found an inside table by the window, from where Via could admire the deep azure blue of the sea against the dramatically formed harsh grey cliffs around the curved coast.

As Lisa had implied, the café was busy, and many of the patrons were young, good-looking, skinny teenagers with olive skin and trendy designer T-shirts, very cool and confident. Very young. Via had got used to the blatant Italian curiosity by then, so the stares of the local kids did not disturb her. What did disturb her was the behavior of the waitress, a pleasant-looking woman in her late twenties who came toward them smiling recognition at Mario, then swung suddenly away again when Giancarlo turned to face her.

She tried to make it look as if she'd forgotten something at the bar, but before she even got there, she answered the call of one of the teenage boys, instead.

"*Persona non grata*, Giancarlo?" Via enquired. "One of your old girlfriends?"

As she spoke, she cast him a wicked look of derision, then wanted to cut out her own tongue. She could see at once that her sardonic guess was way wide of the mark. It was only an instant, a fleeting expression of hurt and resignation crossing his dark eyes before he veiled them.

Then, smiling faintly, he said, "Of course not. She's in hiding from the police." He pushed back his chair and stood. "I'll go up."

Instinct propelled Via after him before her brain properly registered the difficulties. She just knew it was one of the things he never talked about, one of the things that twisted him inside. Catching her gaze as he leaned his elbow on the counter, he arched his eyebrow.

"They'll bring it, you know. I don't need help carrying."

"I know." She insinuated herself between him and the bar so that she faced up to him, almost but not quite touching. A slightly wary expression of amusement crossed his face. Drawing a deep breath, Via said, "She didn't mean it, you know. People just don't know what to say, whether to ask after your health or make jokes or offer sympathy."

She knew he would close her out. She saw it in the quick hardening of his eyes.

"They don't understand," she blurted desperately, "that their embarrassment is so *trivial*. Or perhaps they do, and that's why they're too ashamed to face you."

Though his eyes didn't leave hers, they seemed almost to twitch. Several emotions flickered there at once and were gone, leaving them heart-numbingly softened and, astonishingly, teasing.

"Aren't *you* embarrassed, then, wise woman?"

Just this once, she let herself smile back. "I got over that part of my own triviality a long time ago. Where you are concerned, I appear to be shameless."

It was deliberate, dangerous flirting, and—the sudden self-knowledge left her breathless—it wasn't all done to ease his hurt. His hurt, in fact, was all that gave her the courage. A gleam lit his intense face, a spark of lust that lifted rather than frightened her.

"I wish," he murmured, shifting his elbow on the counter so he could reach her lips with his finger. Suddenly Via became aware of her breasts, hard-tipped and tingling and almost brushing against him. Giancarlo leaned across the tiny distance, and heat flooded her at the touch of his body. Excitement rose quickly, as if they were alone. Under his finger, her lips parted.

Stuff it, I don't care if he was a total bastard. I want him, and I can make him want me. I can do this, I can make him happy, I know I can...

Her pulse raced. Deliberately, she leaned into him, letting him feel the pebbly hardness of her nipples, taking her own pleasure from the stiffening cock against her hip. She heard his breath catch. His hand moved, trailing his finger across her jaw so he could cup her cheek.

"Via. Via, you will wreck me," he whispered.

Just kiss me. Oh, God, please kiss me now...

There might have been no one else in the café, no loud teenagers or interested family observers. Lifting her head provocatively, she closed her lips to wet them with the tip of her tongue and parted them again in open invitation. His head bent closer, and her stomach flipped several somersaults. She felt like moaning with sheer anticipation, for she well remembered his last kiss, before it all went so disastrously wrong; so strong and sensual and completely overwhelming. And now his lips were so close she could feel his warm breath on hers.

"*Ciao*, Giancarlo!" cried a delighted voice, apparently inches away. Via jumped, and Giancarlo let out a strange sound that might have betokened laughter or frustration, or both. His fingers fell away from her face as he turned toward the bar, offering his hand instead to the man who stood behind it.

"I didn't know you were back. Staying long?"

"Just a few days," Giancarlo answered. "Family reunion. This is Via, by the way, from Scotland. Via—Anzio."

Anzio's eyes gleamed appreciation, making Via blush. But since Giancarlo seemed in no hurry to separate their bodies, she stayed determinedly where she was. If he liked what he felt, she was more than happy to emphasize her physical attractions. And if the hardness in his shorts was any guide—which it was!—he liked.

After a short chat about their respective families, Giancarlo ordered wine and coffee and water and slid his hand down her arm, making her shiver as he took her hand to lead her back to the table. Suddenly, she was ridiculously happy, because she knew Giancarlo wanted her. It wasn't over after all. It was just a little more difficult.

Chapter Seven

Walking back to their table, Via couldn't help but be aware of the grinning observation of Mario and Fabio. *God knows what their reaction would have been if we'd actually kissed!* Giancarlo, however, was looking among the teenagers. She felt him nod once or twice, lift his hand casually, and in return got the odd "*Ciao.*"

With a sudden cold contraction of her tingling stomach, Via realized he was *working.* He was watching those kids, noting who sat with whom, looking for a possible contact. So was this new closeness he'd allowed just part of the cover they needed?

Fear and disappointment gnawed at her until, with relief, she remembered his physical reaction. He might well have refrained initially from pushing her out of his way at the bar, just to maintain their cover, but he couldn't pretend an erection. And it wasn't all wishful thinking that had recognized lust and even a little tenderness in his intense, dark eyes. No, he wanted her.

As they slid back into their seats opposite Mario and Fabio, the knowledge gave her confidence to murmur, "You know these kids?"

"Some of them."

"Are they likely to be involved?"

"One or two."

“Is that why we came here?”

“Of course.”

Via smiled and placed her hand lightly on his cotton-covered thigh. Surprise caught at his breath. Via informed the two opposite, “I’ve met Anzio now.”

Mario grinned. “I’m surprised he could prise his way between you two.”

Via laughed and moved her fingers across Giancarlo’s bare leg, sliding them up inside his shorts. His breath hissed between his teeth. Under her hand, he felt tense. Gently, she massaged the bare skin of his thigh, feeling the strength in every sinew and muscle. Desire pooled wetly between her own legs.

Anzio brought the drinks and stayed to exchange a few words before bustling off again. Via slid her hand up Giancarlo’s inner thigh, feeling the skin warmer and smoother. Under the table, while the others made some joke about the kids on the other side of the room and Fabio poured three glasses of wine, Giancarlo’s hand suddenly covered hers on his thigh. But it didn’t caress. His fingers curled around hers and deliberately drew her hand out of his shorts and up to his crotch. His cock was huge and hard under the thin cotton fabric, making her gasp.

His whole face was ablaze with lust, and he let her see it, throwing it at her with all the force of a hurricane.

“You want to go home right now?” he asked, not troubling to lower his voice. “Try out the springs of my old bed?”

“Giancarlo!” Shocked at so public an announcement, she tried to pull her hand free, but he held it firmly, pressing it harder onto his straining cock until she could feel its engorged veins standing out like ribs. The heat of embarrassment as well as desire now flooded her, while Mario and Fabio looked on, amused. And that only by what they could see *above* the table!

"Don't be coarse, Giancarlo." Mario pretended to disapprove, grinning.

"Sorry." He released her hand, turning instead to whisper in her ear. "If you try that again, I'll take you into the toilet and do you there."

She had a glimpse of his eyes, so intense they frightened her. Lust and fury and something else she couldn't fathom glared into her. It didn't help that she was visited by a sudden vision of him "doing her" up against a cubicle wall with her knickers round her ankles, his mouth grinding hers, his big hands kneading her buttocks as he pounded her. Although most of her was far too afraid to go anywhere with him in this mood, some part longed for the wicked experience he so contemptuously offered. It confused her, and he must have seen the mixed feelings in her eyes, for something leapt in his own.

Abruptly he drew away and pushed back his chair to stand.

"Now, if you like," he invited and, with a blatant wink, walked away between the tables to the corner under the sign marked *Toilette.*

Via let her breath out in a rush of relief. She felt as if she'd been run over by a steamroller. Yet still she watched his enticing, tight buttocks swing across the room, and her imagination followed him. Shaking herself free of the torrid visions, she felt like laughing. Excitement grew in her because she understood that, despite appearances, this new mood of his didn't stem from contempt for her, or even from the angry reaction of a puritan. He wanted her, probably as much as she wanted him, and for some reason thought he couldn't, or shouldn't, have her. Which went back to the hang-ups about his illness that she was quite prepared, indeed was determined, to break down.

Dragging her gaze back to the anxious faces of her two companions, she reached defensively for her wine glass.

"Don't be put off by his sense of humor," Mario pleaded.

"I'm not."

"He's had a rough time over the last year."

"I know. I think you all have."

There was relief in Mario's boyish face. "We weren't even sure you knew," he confided. "But he looks so much better. The doctors seem to think now there is reasonable hope. And between you and me, Via, I can't imagine life without him."

Neither can I. The strength of that thought closed up her throat with fear. *Jesus, can I really deal with this?*

It was difficult not to watch for his return. As the minutes passed and there was a lull in the conversation, Via turned casually and saw him standing by one of the teenagers' tables. A boy had stood and was talking to him respectfully enough. A moment later, she saw Giancarlo smile and walk back toward them. She straightened, reaching for her empty glass. Fabio refilled it.

"Thanks," she said as Giancarlo slid into the seat beside her. Deliberately, it seemed, he sat close to her, arms and legs touching, making those butterflies dance again in her stomach. And yet, despite his physical closeness, there was an aura of coldness, of sheer distance around him. He was acting.

Only as they finally left the café did she have a chance to ask him about the youth he'd been talking to earlier.

"Roberto?" he answered. "The nephew of an old friend."

"Oh. I thought perhaps he might be one of those you suspected."

"Not here," he suggested, taking her arm to step on to the

pavement, although he robbed the words of admonishment by adding in her ear, "And he is. Also, he's unhappy. I think he wants to talk to me."

Glancing over her shoulder to make sure they weren't overheard, she said, "He knows you're Carabinieri?"

"Everybody knows. They also know I'm on sick leave and here with my girlfriend."

"And *his* friends?"

He shrugged. "Will know that, too, if they're interested. I don't care for some of his company, and to be honest, I don't think he does, either."

"So, what do we do now?"

"Wait for him to come to me. And if he doesn't, I'll go scare him up. In the meantime, how do you fancy a boat trip tomorrow?"

Via regarded him sardonically. "I'm not being asked on a date here, am I? Where are we going?"

"To the Cinque Terre. Very picturesque. I thought we'd have lunch in a village called Manarola. I know of an excellent restaurant."

"Who frequents it?" Via asked, resigned.

"Marinuzzi," said Giancarlo, looking down at her.

A jolt passed through her, spreading panic and the fear she thought she'd conquered. Swallowing, she said, "Oh."

"I won't leave you," he promised. "He can't hurt you, Via." As if he couldn't help it, his hand lifted, brushing against her cheek in quick reassurance. "But we need him to know you're here, and I'm not sure he'll hear it quickly enough from Roberto and his buddies, if they're even involved in this..."

It gave her plenty to think about on the walk back. But oddly, by the time they reached the house, her panic had died, leaving only a manageable echo of her earlier fear. What she chiefly remembered was that unexpectedly tender caress.

As they entered the gate, Via's attention was caught and held again by the round tower. It had ornamental crenellations and glassless windows beneath. "Can you go up there?" she asked.

"Oh, yes," said Mario, who was just behind her. "The spiral staircase to Giancarlo's room, where you're sleeping, leads up there. We used to play castles and knights in it when we were kids."

"Be a shame not to."

"Giancarlo will show you," Mario offered as they crossed the gravel drive to the front door.

"Thanks, Giancarlo," Via said at once, smiling up at him as she sailed through the door. His expression was both sardonic and resigned.

Half an hour later, they stood together at the top of the tower. Giancarlo leaned his arms across one of sills, looking out over the sea, while Via flitted from place to place to get every view she could.

"What a brilliant place to play," she enthused, coming at last to stand with him. "I'd say you definitely got the best room."

"Privilege of the eldest."

Via leant her arms next to his, making sure they touched, though she didn't look at him as she remarked, "They all think we came up here for a good night kiss."

"I know they do."

She felt his gaze on her, but though she held her breath, he made no move toward her. Nor did he speak. *Bugger. Do I have to do everything?*

She let out a slightly unsteady sigh. Then, turning to him

before she lost the courage, she placed both her hands on his shoulders. "Where is it then?" she asked softly. "Where's my kiss?"

His eyes closed, but his hands fell loosely to his sides without holding her. Gathering courage, she reached up to trace the shape of his full, sculpted lips. At her first touch, his eyes flew open again, revealing lust and longing as well as something that came perilously close to panic.

"Via, don't do this to us. We've been here before. We both know that if I kiss you I won't stop."

"You did the last time," she pointed out. She became fascinated by the way his lips fit together when he stopped speaking and slowly ran her finger along the joining line. When they parted again, she slid it into his mouth and he gasped, catching at her hand and holding it still between them. With trepidation and triumph, she felt the trembling of his whole body, yet he spoke quite steadily with a calm trace of rueful amusement.

"That was last week, and you have no idea how much of my willpower it used up. Besides, I limped all the way home."

"Serves you right."

"I know."

"Is that an apology?"

"No. I want you to remember I'm a bastard."

"Then you owe me," Via murmured, pressing into him, her parted lips turned up to him in open invitation. Oh yes, he was hard already. She was right. "And I want my kiss," she whispered.

"No, you don't," he said sadly. "And you don't want what will come after. I saw it in your eyes the night of our awful date. All you feel is something unfinished between us, and that will go in time."

"You're wrong," she said, clenching her fist against his chest. "Okay, I was taken by surprise. Illness wasn't something I associated with you, and of course I wouldn't want you to be ill again. There's nothing unnatural in that."

"No. But you can't sleep with someone, have sex with someone, from pity. *That* is unnatural."

She stared up at him, feeling it slipping away from her again, unable to reach him to bring it back, yet refusing to let go. "Since when," she asked, "does pity have to be separate from all other feelings? Yes, it would be a pity if you died! For what it's worth, you don't look like dying to me. And also for what it's worth, I wanted *you*. I knew there could be something special between us, before I knew anything about your illness. I wanted you the night we met, remember? I could talk myself into thinking that was shock, dependence, whatever, but when we met again, I knew it wasn't those things. Giancarlo, either of us could be dead tomorrow, run over by a bus. Or drowned at sea off the Cinque Terre."

He spared a faint smile for that one, but the distance was still there. Though he continued to hold her hand between their bodies, apart from that he didn't touch her.

Via took a deep breath. "Giancarlo, I'm not used to... *pursuing* men. I've never done it in my life before, if you want the truth, and I don't want to become a... *a stalker*. So if you look into my eyes and tell me honestly that you don't want me, I won't come near you again."

Giancarlo moved, putting both his hands heavily on her shoulders. His eyes looked straight into hers, but though his gaze was steady, his expression was not. A thousand storms and battles waged in those intense eyes, including lust and anger, longing and revulsion, tenderness and cruelty.

"Via," he said, "I don't want you."

It hurt. She couldn't pretend it didn't. She had to pull herself out of his hold, turning her back so that she faced the wonderful view blindly.

"Yes, but that wasn't honest, was it, Giancarlo?"

For a moment, there was silence. She thought miserably that he might even have left the room. Then she felt him stir behind her.

"No," he said at last. "It wasn't honest."

She hadn't expected him to admit it so easily, and turned to confront him, forgetting the wetness of her eyes.

"Christ, Via, don't cry! Of course I want you. I'd have to be blind and deaf and totally numb below the waist not to want you. But I don't want you *like this!*"

"Like *what*?" she demanded. "Where is the difference between *this* and the day we met at the café in Pisa? You wanted me then, you'd have made love to me then!"

"A one-night stand," he said cruelly. "That's what I wanted. A night of fun and passion. I didn't want to marry you."

"Who proposed? So what's wrong *now* with a night of fun and passion?"

Abruptly, he turned away from her, sweeping one hand over his shaven head before swinging back to say, "It wouldn't be one night, though, would it? It's beyond that. Perhaps it always was, I don't know. You have...expectations that..."

"That what?"

"That appeal," he said with difficulty, then, as if he saw the hope leaping in her eyes, added, "on some level. But that I can't fulfill. I can't have a relationship. I don't want one, and neither do you, not this one. I'm a bastard. That's not the cancer, I was always a bastard. Ask Angelina. I'm difficult and moody and selfish beyond belief, and I can be cruel for no reason that means a damn to anybody else. You already know that. If I was *well*, any friend would tell you to think bloody carefully before you went out with me. But I'm not well, and perhaps I never will be. Even if I am, God knows what the chemotherapy has done to me. Let's say I'm unlikely to be family man.

"And if I'm *not* well... Via, neither of us wants you to be a nurse. And neither of us wants you to walk away because you can't bear it anymore. I couldn't stand that again, and I don't think you could endure the guilt."

His words hammered into her, as he meant them to, hurting, wounding, driving her away. Right until the end, when her bowed head came up and she stared at him.

I couldn't stand that again.

He knew he'd made a mistake. His expression told her before he swung away, clearly determined to leave this time. But she darted after him, catching his arm.

"Is that what happened?" she whispered. "Did someone walk away when you were ill?"

Though he didn't look at her, he did stand still. "We'd been living together for a year. It was fun. Perhaps I thought it was more. It stopped being fun when they found the tumor. I don't blame her. And I wouldn't blame you. It's just... I can't, I *won't* put my trust in anyone until I know I'm well. It wouldn't be fair, least of all to you. You don't need someone else dying on you."

"No," she agreed, "I don't. But we both need to *live*, for whatever time's left to us, sixty years or six weeks."

His arm jerked in her hold, though he wouldn't turn in answer to her tugging. She swung round to face him.

"You think that's trite? It isn't, not for anybody. Giancarlo, I can't promise never to leave you. All I can swear is, that if I do, it won't be because you're ill."

Slowly, his anguished gaze came down to hers, a strong, independent man trying desperately to hide his pain, his fear. She longed to reach up, to hold him, but she knew instinctively it would be the wrong thing to do. Her lips twisted in a sardonic smile.

"Actually, the likeliest reason is your being a complete arse."

Surprised laughter hissed between his teeth. She let her own eyes smile back. "So what do you say? Do I get my kiss?"

There was a pause. Via's heart beat and beat. At last, slowly, his arms lifted. One big hand took hold of her tangled hair, pushing it carefully back behind her shoulder. Then his arms closed loosely about her, bent at the elbows; both hands held her face and he leaned toward her. She was afraid to move, to breathe, in case she scared him off again.

Very gently, his mouth touched her parted lips, brushing them, then slowly, tenderly sinking into them.

I would die for this kiss.

Yet before she could open wider to him, he was already releasing her. "I'm not worth it," he whispered. "Good night."

And his hands fell away, leaving her cold and bereft. Once again, he walked away from her, closing the door softly behind him.

Chapter Eight

From the first moment of waking, thinking, inevitably, of her, Giancarlo forced his mind to keep busy on work, checking sailing times and the various routes from the village of Manarola up to Marinuzzi's house, just in case they had to take a country walk to be seen.

Giancarlo had few illusions. He knew he was taking Via into the lion's den, setting her up, and he knew he was her only protection. He also knew that Marinuzzi's organization extended to rather more than a few alienated kids heavily into devil worship. There were connections to organized crime as well as to Satanist cults, and Giancarlo's mind was still open as to whether he used the Satanism to control his organization, or whether he genuinely believed these grotesque rituals would bring him more power. Since discovering Marinuzzi's deliberate targeting of Via, he was inclining toward the latter, although how any grown man with his sanity intact could actually believe that stuff was beyond him. He'd had differences of opinion on this general subject with his colleagues before he'd gone off on sick leave, but since their views mattered to him, he couldn't discount them entirely.

He let his mother fuss over getting him breakfast and coffee, then dragged her off with him to sit outside while he ate it. She seemed so pleased with his company that he immediately began to feel guilty again. But her anxiety, her fear, oppressed him, and he was very well aware that much as he loved her, if this thing with Marinuzzi had not come up, he wouldn't have come home.

He needed to work.

"Admire the stars last night?" Lisa smirked as she wandered out to join them.

"Yes, thank you," Giancarlo said peacefully.

His sister rubbed her hand across his smooth head. "I like her. She's smart and prickly and doesn't take any shit from you."

"Lisa," Antonia reproved.

Lisa laughed. "Well, she doesn't. Most of his women let him walk all over them."

"You make it sound as if he has a harem."

Giancarlo said, "Would you like me to go so you can discuss me without my inconvenient presence?"

"No, no, Giancarlo, we don't regard your presence at all," Lisa assured him, grinning, just as Via came out of the kitchen door and into the sunlight. Dressed in simple, cropped white trousers and a sun top that only just met them, she nevertheless had the effect of dazzling Giancarlo. As usual when he caught sight of her, his heart gave its warning thud, his loins began to stir, and he had difficulty keeping his eyes off her.

She didn't look at him, though. She said a general "*Buonjuorno,*" but gave her direct smile to his mother, with a quick echo for Lisa. Only as she sat, and Antonia began to pour her a cup of coffee, did her gaze flicker to Giancarlo. He had a glimpse of embarrassment, no doubt associated with their conversation last night and her blatant plea for his kiss. And more.

He started to smile, a rueful twist of the lips that was meant to soothe. But as soon as it began, she glanced away, flushing. Fiercely, selfishly, Giancarlo gloried in his effect on her. Since his teenage years, he'd been used to attracting women, took it for granted. Yet for some reason Via's desire, her inability to deal with his physical presence, moved him beyond belief, tugging at his own predatory instincts so that he wanted to hunt her down. He wanted to entice her away from his mother's breakfast table to some quiet corner where he could take her in his arms, touch her, feel her heated body tremble with need for his. He wanted to kiss her breathless, take both of her pert, naked breasts in his hands and fuck her senseless. Not for the first time, he was desperate to know how she would feel clinging to his hard cock as he pushed it inside her. Would she moan and whimper as she reached for her pleasure, or was she the screaming type?

Well, you'll never know, he told himself savagely as he surreptitiously adjusted his position to try to cover the raging erection now tenting his shorts.

Giancarlo had grown up here, had been sailing between his hometown and the Cinque Terre since childhood. Yet doing it now in a tourist ship, seeing it through Via's eyes, everything seemed quite new. The battered little boats out fishing on the clear, azure water, bobbing alongside swish motorboats and passenger ships, began to take on new character. The constantly changing coast around spectacular bay after bay was interesting again. Terraces of vines gave way to rolling, tree-covered hills rising above Roman ruins. Simple, ever-present things he'd long taken for granted were suddenly charming because she saw them, too.

Gradually, she appeared to forget her tension, both at his presence and at the possible ordeal ahead of her, in the sheer beauty of the coastline and the charming, colorful villages perched high on the cliffs.

"Wow," she said in awe as the ship chugged into the little harbor at Manarola. "You grew up surrounded by such beauty. And I bet you never even noticed."

He shrugged. "I liked the sea. But I suppose I took the rest for granted. Didn't you? Wasn't there beauty where you grew up?"

"Maybe," she allowed. "We lived at the coast, too, but it isn't spectacular like this." She shivered in remembrance. "A lot colder, for one thing, and the sea is generally grey."

Climbing the steps over the cliff from the harbor, Giancarlo unthinkingly took her hand to steady her. To his secret delight, it jumped nervously in his hold, though she let it lie there. He could almost see her remembering that they had to play the part of lovers. It was cruel to do this to her, he supposed.

Well, where would be the harm? a voice whispered in his head. *She wants it, you want it. What would be wrong with a night of passion?*

Nothing. Except she'd been right, back in Pisa. There'd always been more between them. Just not enough to get them through the next year. There was never enough for that.

At the top of the steps was a café, where they stopped to have coffee and ice cream. Or at least Via had the ice cream, while Giancarlo enjoyed watching her. Once, as her tongue snaked around the peaked ice cream in the cone, her eyes met his and gleamed. Her confidence was back. She was definitely flirting again. And he couldn't help smiling in return, despite the sudden ache in his shorts.

They spent the rest of the morning wandering round the village, climbing up the steep hill to the medieval church, looking in tourist shops, taking photographs. Although Via seemed to forget why they were here, Giancarlo's guard never dropped. Constantly on the lookout for their quarry or for anybody who looked remotely interested in Via, he could not and would not relax. Only when he took her hand, this time for the benefit of their cover, did she glance at him as if she felt his tension and remembered her own.

"Lunch time, I think," Giancarlo murmured, and her fingers gripped his convulsively. "All right?"

She nodded, smiling quickly, and though he gave her a moment to back out, she didn't take it, or even seem to notice it. His heart warmed toward her afresh. He could feel her fear, her memory, almost as sharply as if they were his, but she wouldn't bow to them. She would do her bit to catch the murderous bastard.

Marinuzzi wasn't there. To relax her, Giancarlo kept up a flow of conversation, occasionally distracting her or making her laugh, sometimes flirting just to see her blush, although she clearly believed he only did it to lend color to their pretense.

At last, unable to stay longer without drawing attention to them, Giancarlo paid the bill and suggested a walk. Nervously, Via agreed. It was just when they stood to go that the door opened once again, and a shadow blotted out the sun.

Marinuzzi. If Giancarlo didn't know him already from photographs, Via's sudden paralysis would have told him.

Not a particularly tall man, nor a well built one, but certainly a man with presence, even in the casual slacks and shirt he wore. In his late forties, Giancarlo guessed, and still in his prime. His voice boomed confidently across the restaurant, booking a table for four for that evening, and received a swift, respectful acknowledgement.

When it seemed he would actually turn and leave without

noticing them, Giancarlo said quickly, "Via, have you got your bags?" It didn't matter what he said. The name held all the importance necessary, and it had its desired effect.

Marinuzzi turned his head back into the room, unerringly finding Via, who stood frozen in his gaze like a rabbit in headlights. Giancarlo took her hand, and she shrank against him. "Via?" he said, allowing concern to seep into his tones.

"Via," Marinuzzi said blankly, then an instant later he was moving toward them.

Via's fear was no pretense. Giancarlo could almost smell it. He put his left arm around her, leaving his right free to deal with Marinuzzi if he had to. But the bastard was all conciliation. In English.

"*Signorina*, you'll never know how appalled I am that such a thing could have happened to you, so soon after leaving our employ, too. My boys are too high-spirited..."

"Your boys are psychos," Via interrupted. Though her voice shook, Giancarlo was so proud of her he wanted to laugh in the older man's face. Marinuzzi's cold, grey eyes flashed.

In Italian, Giancarlo said, "This is the father of the men who assaulted you?"

Via nodded. He could feel her trembling and gripped her shoulder. "Then you'll forgive us if we don't stay to chat," he said frigidly. "Via has been through enough."

"I quite understand," said Marinuzzi, but he didn't stand aside. Instead, looking hard at Via, he said, "You should have come to us afterwards. Not remained alone in a foreign country after such a dreadful thing."

"To be honest I have found being alone far preferable to being with your family."

Again his eyes flashed, but this time Via didn't wait around to see it. She all but pushed past Marinuzzi, swiftly making for the door. Giancarlo followed so that no real distance was ever between them, yet as he held the door open for her, she suddenly stopped dead, staring straight ahead of her. Two, maybe three seconds passed, long enough for Giancarlo to frown with sudden anxiety.

"Via?"

"Jesus," she whispered, and bolted out of the shop. Giancarlo had to run to catch her, grasping her arm in genuine concern.

"Via, what is it? Why...?"

"Let's just get as far away from here as possible," she said tightly. Her voice shook. Her whole body shook.

Giancarlo swept his arm around her shoulders and walked with her down the hill. "Come on," he said. "I'll take you along the Via del Amore."

She stared up at him. A quick, unsteady laugh broke from her. "You're a sick bastard," she said.

He smiled and dropped a kiss on the top of her head. What he wanted to do was take her in his arms and kiss all of her, drive away whatever had frightened her so badly, protect her from all the scum of the world.

They were actually on the walk, a spectacular pathway carved into the cliff face around the coast between Manarola and Riomaggiore, the next village along, before she spoke again. Even then, it was only to say abruptly, "They carve their names in the plants?"

"Plants, trees, stone, all, anything," Giancarlo answered, following her gaze to the cactus that had attracted her attention. Its long, flat leaves were covered in hearts and names and initials, all cut into their flesh.

Via kept walking. She said, “Is your name here?”

“I don’t imagine so. If it is, I didn’t put it there.”

Though she didn’t look at him, she smiled faintly over the foliage to the sea. “Not even when you were young and romantic?”

“I was born old and cynical.”

Now she looked at him, and her eyes were disconcertingly clear and shrewd. “No you weren’t. You talk a lot of crap sometimes.”

Surprised, he could only blink and hope he would be amused later.

“Last night, for example,” she said, standing aside to let another couple go past. “Last night you said you were a bastard and always had been. Well, maybe you behave like one from time to time. Who doesn’t? But a bastard wouldn’t have stopped for me on that road to Pisa, let alone looked after me as you did. Good and strong and kind spring to mind for starters.”

Her green eyes glinted in the sunlight yet remained steadily on his, showing him all her trust and admiration. Warmed by her words in spite of himself, those eyes nearly undid him altogether, for it wasn’t just admiration he read there, it was adoration.

Oh, Jesus, God.

“Accept it,” she said wryly. “I like you.”

Breaking her gaze, he moved on, only realizing when he let it go in a long rush that he’d been holding his breath.

“I can live with like,” he said at last. Then, taking her hand as they moved toward a covered part of the walk, he added, “So trust me. Talk to me. What scared you in the restaurant?”

She didn’t pretend to misunderstand him. Nor did she avoid it, which made him breathe a metaphorical sigh of relief.

Frowning, she looked away, out through the stone arch to where the tiny boats still played on the deep blue water.

"I'm not sure. Now we're away from it, I could almost think I imagined it. I...I thought I heard him in my head."

As if she consciously plucked up the courage, she lifted her chin. "He said... I thought he said, *'I'm coming for you; I'll get you this time'*."

Her hand twisted in Giancarlo's as if she saw the doubt raging through his anger. He held on to it, drawing her closer again so he could put his arm round her waist.

"You think I've finally lost it," she said in a small, tight voice. She felt stiff as a rod, for the first time ever unresponsive to his touch. The hurt, the disappointment of that, took him by surprise.

"No," he objected, hugging her to his side. God, she was soft and enticing, even when she tried to be unyielding. "Of course I believe you. Has anything like this ever happened to you before?"

She began to shake her head at once, then paused, gazing along the cliffs as if not really seeing them. At last she said, "I'm not sure. Never so clear and never so scary. Maybe it's a bit like the dreams I can never quite remember 'til something happens and everyone tells me my feeling of familiarity is just déjà vu. Sometimes, I think people have said something, and they haven't. I hear a voice, and when I turn round, there's no one near me."

Giancarlo felt a shiver run up his spine. For once it was a relief to go out of the shade into the full heat of the summer sun.

"Once," Via said, smiling faintly, "I was at this party talking to a girl I'd never met before. I thought she made some remark along the lines of 'God, he's beautiful, I really wouldn't mind him in my knickers.' And I said...this bloke she was eyeing up was a huge, chunky, rugby-player type, by the way. I knew him slightly. So I said, 'You'd need some of Bridget Jones's Big Pants to accommodate him.' I thought I was being quite witty—I'd had a few—but this poor girl went bright pink with embarrassment and practically ran away from me. According to everyone else, she hadn't said anything at all about this guy to me, and, even worse, he was going out with her best friend."

"Oops," Giancarlo said, vaguely amused while part of him still tried to rationalize and account for such phenomena. Aloud, he theorized, "It's as if you have some *echo* of a gift, or a gift that isn't properly realized. Marinuzzi wants it."

"But Marinuzzi must have a gift of his own if he can speak to me like that."

"Maybe he didn't speak to you. Maybe he was just like the girl at the party and *thinking*. But in this case he was thinking about *you*."

As he had meant her to be, she seemed a little happier with this explanation. Not surprisingly, the idea Marinuzzi was deliberately frightening her by speaking inside her head had freaked her out badly.

The boat that took them back from Riomaggiore was the last of the day and very crowded. Giancarlo elbowed them some standing room at the back, where they leaned their arms on the rail and let the beauty of the scenery wash over them with the heat of the sun. For no reason, Giancarlo felt good. Her arm was touching his, her warmth seeping through the short sleeve of his shirt, brushing the bare skin of his lower arm, and he liked the low-level electricity of that. He liked being with her, feeling her close, looking at her. He enjoyed her swift, constantly-changing expressions as she drank in the beauty of her surroundings or dragged the hair out of her face for the breeze to blow back again almost immediately. Her laughter made him smile; her smile melted his bones. When she turned to speak to him and her breast brushed against his arm, a hot spurt of desire curled through him. And yet the pleasure was in doing nothing about it. The pleasure was in her.

Responding to his light, easy questions, she told him a little of her life in Scotland, her friends and family, until at last he realized it was the right moment to ask. Yet still he hesitated, afraid to spoil the unexpected contentment that had sprung up between them.

Feeling his gaze, she glanced at him through her hair and smiled. "What?"

"I was wondering when your parents died." *Too curt, moron!*

The smile faded, but naturally. "My father, when I was fourteen. He'd left years before, though. He was in Australia with his new family when he got ill. Bowel cancer. We never saw him again. My mother died a couple of years ago. Of lung cancer."

"I'm sorry," he said inadequately.

"Yes, so was she. She'd stopped smoking years before, but the damage was done. We tried to nurse her at home, but it was too cruel. She needed constant care at the end, constant changes in the drug dosages to keep the pain at bay, so she went into a hospice."

Though her eyes seemed to have grown bigger and she wouldn't look at him, she did not cry. "Two months after she died, my oldest friend died of breast cancer. She left two kids and a husband who had adored her since she was fourteen."

His breath caught. He couldn't not put his arm round her, rest his chin on the top of her head. It was sweet, exquisite pain to realize he was right, that she had borne enough.

"She lived for the day," Via said quietly. "From the moment she knew, she made sure none of them stopped living, living *with her.*"

It wasn't a lecture, but it got to him as it was meant to. The contentment began to slip into a buzz of conjecture, temptation and possibilities, and the pause went on too long, much too long, before he said, "You've known more grief than most."

"I've known more fun and affection, too."

"And more about cancer."

Her smile was twisted as she pulled back from his embrace. "Let's say I don't smoke, I check my breasts every month and I never need to be reminded twice to get my cervical smear test. I'm not paranoid, I just take sensible precautions. Your knowledge is first-hand, though."

And before he knew how, although he hadn't meant to do it, he was talking about his own illness, the weakness, the blinding headaches, the torture of waiting for diagnosis, of dealing with the fears of his family by keeping his own in check. Then the change that came with the operation and the awful, debilitating chemotherapy that had made his hair fall out. The deliberate effort to rebuild his normal health and strength, his desperation to go back to work, to fill the time until his next test, if for no other reason. To stop him thinking.

To all of this she listened, nodding occasionally. But although she held his hand as she'd been doing since he'd first taken hers and occasionally squeezed his fingers, she showed no overt sympathy or pity, just an *understanding* that was singularly sweet.

And when the boat finally docked and the passengers began to disembark, she glanced at him and smiled, saying something about his mother's cooking that he barely heard. His head, his whole being, was full of emotion, full of her. Because he'd found her, his One, as he would have known two weeks ago if he'd let himself.

Of course, it made no difference. Not now. But, maybe later. Maybe, if he survived the next year, they could meet again.

Make her wait that long? How cruel was that? Especially when he knew what he did to her. What he'd deliberately done to her in Pisa. He owed her for that alone.

But maybe there was a way to pay that debt. All it took was strength.

In his darkroom, where he pretended to develop black and white photographs, Arturo Marinuzzi closed the book with an excited snap. The next two nights would be good. At last, there was hope. Standing, he went to the door and put out the light before leaving.

At last, after some hopeless days, things were looking up. His sons were charged with assault and murder, and there had seemed nothing he could do about that. Too many people were beyond bribery, and his powers of coercion were just not powerful enough to work on anyone with any strength of mind. Not yet. But now...!

Via! The word from Scotland had been right after all. He was almost sure of it now. When she'd frozen in the restaurant doorway, her back to him, something had radiated from her, something intense and far more than simple fear, though there was that, too. It was almost as if she'd heard his vicious mental promise to get her. That peculiar idea had stayed with him all through the drive home, and now, with much reading and more thought, he was sure he was right. She *had* heard him, she *was* gifted, and for the next two nights the planetary positions were auspicious for the Evil One. Such a sacrifice at such a time would surely enable him not only to free his stupid boys, but drastically improve his business—that Roman take-over, for example.

Oh, yes, now she was definitely worth the risk. It no longer mattered a hang that she was with the sick policeman. Not, Marinuzzi thought regretfully, that he'd appeared very sick to him. On the contrary, he'd looked extremely strong and formidably intelligent, a worthy opponent, perhaps, in other circumstances. But in matters of the occult, as Marinuzzi had discovered, Giancarlo Di Ripoli was well known among his colleagues as a profound skeptic. Marinuzzi's powers and those he could gain from the girl were way over the policeman's head.

"Giovanni," he called, pushing open his son's bedroom door. Though the boy was asleep, he sat up immediately, wide-eyed and at least pretending alertness. "Get the local kids together again. Tomorrow night. And the one after. This is big."

Chapter Nine

Despite the very real fear engendered by her brief encounter with Marinuzzi, Via found she was able to put it to the back of her mind quite easily. Instead, her wayward thoughts dwelled on Giancarlo and the definite breaking down of the barriers between them. They were false barriers, anyway, erected by Giancarlo for his own protection as well his misplaced concern for hers. But this afternoon, on the ship, they'd certainly weakened, and the knowledge infused Via with new hope.

Butterflies danced excitedly in her stomach as she undressed and showered before dinner. The hot jets of water coursed down her skin, sensitizing every nerve in her body, tightening her nipples until they peaked hard and prominent. She wondered how long she would have to wait for his touch there now. Not very, if she had anything to do with it.

She smiled to herself, turning so the water could run between her legs, cleansing her of the moisture her body leaked so continuously when she was near him. It was a losing battle. She was thinking of him now, imagining him here with her, maybe even tonight when the house was quiet, soaping her all over with his big, tender hands, pinching sensually at those pebbled nipples, rocking his erection between her legs while she pushed into him, holding his firm, tight buttocks as she longed to, reaching up to kiss his full, oh so desirable lips. He would taste of…

Via, stop it! She broke into her own thoughts severely. *At the very least, you have to eat dinner with his parents first, make polite conversation. How are you going to do that if you're so turned on you're* wriggling*?*

At least that image made her giggle. She turned off the shower, stepped out and wrapped herself in the big white towel she'd brought down from her bedroom. Leaving the bathroom and climbing the spiral staircase to her own room, she began to plan what she would wear to seduce Giancarlo away from his erroneous sense of honor. The white linen dress probably looked best, but she rather thought it held bad connotations for him now. The bright orange one, she decided with satisfaction. She rarely wore it because the neck was a little too low to be comfortable, but tonight, she reckoned, called for desperate measures.

Humming happily to herself, she wandered into her bedroom and closed the door. And stopped dead in her tracks.

Giancarlo stood by the window, already changed into yet more casual shorts and a loose white shirt. Though he must have heard her coming, he stood with his back to her, giving her just a moment to calm the sudden jolt of her heart, to admire the breadth of his shoulders and the length of his bare, powerful legs.

She let her breath out slowly, hoping her voice wouldn't shake. *Don't blow this, Via. This is the best chance you'll have.*

"Giancarlo."

He turned, and Via remembered in panic that she hadn't so much as combed out her hair, just toweled it dry so it probably stuck up round her head like a clown's. But Giancarlo didn't laugh. She thought his breath shuddered as their eyes met. His gaze dropped to her lips and lower and kept going, roving all over her. Via clutched at her towel.

Swallowing, she managed to say, "You have me at a disadvantage."

"Yes, I do, don't I?" he agreed, and began to walk toward her with purposeful, predatory steps.

Again her heart lurched. She'd determined to seduce him, and now it seemed she didn't have to try, not if the expression in his hot, dark eyes was anything to go by as he came to a halt in front of her, close but not touching. Lust blazed out of them, igniting her own desire afresh.

Don't count your chickens. You've been here before, she warned herself. Yet still, those eyes, the sensual smile curling his lip, gave her the confidence to provoke him. "Something I can do for you, Giancarlo?"

His smile widened and slowly died. His hand rose to cover hers where it clutched the towel above her breast.

"Yes. Drop the towel."

Heat suffused her whole body. Her legs began to tremble. Obediently, she let go of the towel, sliding her hand free, so that for an instant it was Giancarlo who held it closed around her. Then with one tug, he freed the ends, and it fell to the floor round her feet.

She wanted to close her eyes, afraid of reading dissatisfaction or disappointment in his eyes. Her breasts were too small, her hips too wide, and there was that ugly mole on her pelvis...

"Christ. You're so beautiful I'm almost afraid to touch you. In case you shatter."

He whispered the words in Italian, causing her eyes to fly open wide to see if she'd heard aright. His whole face seemed to smolder, drinking her in like wine.

“Shatter me, Giancarlo,” she pleaded. “Please don’t be afraid of that...”

Quick laughter hissed between his teeth. “I said ‘*almost* afraid’.” His big hands reached up, closing on her shoulders, drawing her that extra step until she rested against him, feeling the warmth of his body through his clothes, the hard ridge of his cock at her hip. He bent his head slowly and kissed her mouth.

Remembering, she kept her eyes open this time so she could see the desire and the delight in his. Sensation washed over her, the firm, warm texture of his lips moving across hers, opening them for his pleasure, his eyes boring into hers, wanting her. She gasped into his mouth, throwing her arms around his neck, pressing her naked body into him, wriggling until she felt the hardness of his cock against her pubic bone, then standing on tip-toe so it reached lower, between her legs.

His arms swept round her, holding her there as he delved into her mouth He slid his tongue along the length of hers, twisting them together like an erotic dance. Via moaned, opening wider for him, drawing him in. The kiss deepened impossibly as his hands slid down her back to her buttocks, caressing, kneading, holding them steady so he could grind into her.

Never in her life had Via been so turned on by a kiss. Every tingle, every pleasurable sensation seemed to be heightened by watching herself in his eyes and reading there what she did to him.

He broke it at last, only to lift her in his arms as if she were a baby and carry her the few paces to the narrow bed. There he laid her down, and she watched with hot impatience as he tore off his shirt. Her arms reached for him even before it was over his head, and he smiled, lowering himself into her embrace, with one big hand closing over her breast.

It felt so good, so right there, that she laid her own over it, holding it to her, making him smile before he slanted his mouth across hers and kissed her again. Caressing her breast, he played with her nipple, stroked it into a hard peak with rough and tender fingers. Via twisted against him, pressing her hot pussy into his leg.

With a kind of groaning sigh, Giancarlo left her mouth. He traced a line of hot, sensual kisses down her throat and shoulder. She arched up to him, pleading for more. His lips closed around her nipple. Moaning at the feel of his tongue, his teeth, she ran her hands across his naked shoulders and back, pushing against the waistband of his shorts. He didn't help her, just went on kissing and pulling at her breast, building a wild fever of pleasure and need in her. With a final flick of his wicked tongue, he left her nipple and moved to the other breast. At the same time, his hand swept down across her stomach, his finger pushing suggestively at her navel. Via pushed back and saw him smile around her breast.

His hand slid lower, edging nearer to the core of heat between her legs. Parting them for him, she lifted her hips, inviting, pleading for his caresses there. At the first touch of his fingers on her pussy, she cried out, almost in relief that the waiting was over. Although he held her there for only the first few moments, the sensations overwhelmed her. She loved his touch; she would die for his touch...

"Sh-sh," he warned teasingly. "You wouldn't want my mother to come up and spoil the fun just yet, would you?"

"God no," she gasped out, almost sobbing as his fingers began to move and explore among the soft, sensitive folds.

"Oh, you're hot down there," he whispered. "Hot and so

incredibly wet. I've made you wait too long."

She moaned again as his fingers found her hard, swollen clitoris, separating it from its enclosing petals and so softly, tenderly rubbing. Her hands scrabbled across his back and shoulders, running down his muscled chest in search of what she craved inside her. He moved, letting her find the ridge of his cock and caress it hard through his shorts. With trembling, anxious fingers, she unbuttoned his fly, freeing the enormous shaft.

He growled deep in his throat as she closed both her hands around it, squeezing.

"I think you've waited too long as well," she whispered.

"It's too big for you," he teased.

"No, it's not," she said with certainty, and tried to sit up, to reach for it with her mouth.

But he held her back, using just one hand while the other continued to work its magic around the bud and petals of her pussy.

"It's time," she urged breathlessly. "Giancarlo, please, come inside me! I want you so badly..."

"Don't you want this?" he asked huskily, sweeping his fingers down the line of her pussy and pressing on her clitoris until she gasped.

"Oh, yes," she breathed fervently, "but I want it to be together..."

"Lie back," he said, "Just lie back and let me pay my debt."

As he spoke, he slipped out of her hold, drawing himself lower down the bed until he could kiss her thighs.

"Oh, God," Via whispered as his tongue snaked around with his fingers, teasing and licking. His lips caressed her petals. Via felt her pussy contract involuntarily, trying to draw him in, and obligingly, he slid one finger inside her. She grasped at his smooth head, whispering his name. His lips closed around her clitoris, just as a second finger joined the first and pushed in and out and in again. Via thrust herself onto them, glorying in the feel of them swirling and plunging inside her. Strange, excited animal sounds, at once anxious and joyful, came from somewhere deep inside her. The pleasure was so overwhelming she thought she might explode before she came. And she was coming. The waves were building, growing, heightening.

He began to suck her clitoris, flicking around it with his tongue, and the waves broke over her with impossible intensity, shattering her into a thousand joyful pieces of absolute pleasure. Yet still he didn't leave her. Holding her bucking hips with his strong hands, he kept caressing her clitoris with his tongue, even pushed one more finger inside her, thrusting hard to keep her climax at its height long beyond anything she'd ever experienced before.

"My God, Giancarlo," she whispered as it began to recede at last. He lifted his head, smiling though his eyes blazed with lust and triumph at what he'd done to her. Breathing erratically, he brought his big body back up to her embrace, pressing his crotch once against her sensitive pussy before quickly lying down beside her again. His hand was back at her pussy, stirring.

Half-laughing, she pulled at him. "Now! I want to see you come."

"I want to see *you* come," he returned at once, his fingers sliding over her slick, sodden folds.

"I just did," she all but sobbed.

"I was too far away to see properly. Again," he said, like a command, and as if her body knew to obey, it fell over the edge once more, racking her in a series of wild, convulsions while he avidly watched her ecstatic face. Even when she couldn't keep the cries of pleasure inside any longer, he only covered her mouth with his to muffle the noise and continued to gaze into her eyes through the kiss.

He tasted of her, as if she'd branded him, although it was he who'd given all the pleasure. She kissed him back, achingly, until the last wave died away. Then, their mouths separating, they smiled at each other.

Via nestled into his embrace. Never in her life had she come so high or been so satisfied. Oh yes, he was definitely the One!

Then, too quickly, Giancarlo observed, "Dinner will be ready. They'll come to look for us soon."

She grinned. "I'm sure we've got enough time."

"Come on," he said, separating, fastening his shorts as he stood. Via rose onto one elbow and cradled her head in her hand, watching him, a little puzzled.

"Later?" she suggested, smiling with all the new confidence he'd given her. But his eyes were veiled again.

He hesitated, then: "No, Via. Not later, either." He sat again, his hand reaching out to her cheek, cupping it. "That was for Pisa. And I loved every moment. But it won't happen again, not until..."

He broke off, his eyes going beyond hers now while his meaning began to penetrate her fog of sexual fulfillment and bewilderment. The silence was palpable.

"You're doing it again," she whispered.

He frowned, his eyes coming back to her. "What?"

"You're doing it again," she repeated, more strongly, more coldly. "Was that really meant to *help* me? Provide a little taste of what I'm missing? How much food does your bloody ego eat?"

"Lots," he said unsteadily, getting to his feet. "Lots and lots."

"And you can really do that? You can walk away now? Like *that*?" She pointed significantly at the huge, tented bulge in his shorts.

"I don't know about walk," he said candidly, shifting position, "but I will certainly hobble."

"No."

"Please, you know you can't stop me."

"I know I can't pull you back physically and make you stay right now. I mean no, you can't walk away from this. You want me too much. You like me too much, and I won't let you waste my life or yours."

The beginnings of anger flashed in his eyes. "My life is not your concern."

"Oh, yes," said Via, "it is."

And without looking at him again, she got off the bed and walked naked across the room in front of him toward the wardrobe. Opening the door, she reached up deliberately to the hanger with the orange dress. The bedroom door opened and quickly closed.

"Shit," Via whispered, resting her head on the wardrobe. "Shit and shit and shit."

Via had never paid much attention to her appearance before. She expected people, including men, to take her as they found her, and if they didn't like her, tough. But that evening, she took extreme care and she knew, with some surprise, that she looked great.

Her hair fell in a burnished cascade around her semi-naked shoulders. The skin of her face glowed through its fetching tan, and her lips, deliberately well-bitten because she'd left the only lipstick she possessed in Pisa, looked alluringly rosy and kissable. The neck of the orange dress revealed enough cleavage to catch anyone's eye and, just in case *he* wasn't looking, she wore her grandmother's antique peridot and diamond pendant to capture his attention. Enticingly, it nestled between her breasts. Then, for the first time since the disastrous date with Giancarlo, she wore the sandals with heels to make her legs look longer. That seemed to work, too.

Examining herself in the wardrobe mirror before going down, she felt tall and elegant and glamorous. Overkill for a quiet family dinner in the garden? Maybe, but there was no way he could ignore her tonight. Tossing her hair back over her shoulder, she sallied forth to the battle.

She met no one on the stairs, which was unfortunate because she thought she looked pretty regal as she descended their wide sweep. *Ah, well, there's always going back up.*

When she entered the kitchen, Antonia's mouth fell open.

"Mama," Lisa exclaimed, hastily taking the casserole from her apparently nerveless fingers. She looked Via up and down with frank approval. "Wow! You look amazing."

"Is Giancarlo being stupid?" Antonia asked, a glimmer of shrewd understanding in her dark eyes.

"Not if I can help it," Via said grimly, and Lisa laughed. "Can I carry the vegetables?"

"No, bring the wine," Lisa advised. "It'll show you off better."

Going out into the garden first, Antonia bustled with the casserole to the foot of the white-clothed table and Lisa veered off toward Fabio. This allowed all the men, lounging over their wine while talking idly, a clear view of Via as she advanced across the terrace, her hips swaying in the clinging silk dress, the bottle swinging casually in her careless grasp.

Fabio's reaction was much like Antonia's. His jaw dropped until Lisa nudged him and he closed it with a snap. Giancarlo's father simply stared for an instant before his lips pursed in a silent whistle and he got to his feet. There was nothing new in this. He was of the old-fashioned school that always stood to greet a woman, only this time he nearly came to grief tripping over Mario, who shot up from his chair like a bat out of hell to show her where to sit.

Smiling at the older man and laughing at Mario, Via laid the wine on the table. This meant she leaned down across Giancarlo. Without looking at him, for now that she was here, basking in the admiration of the other men and even the tolerant understanding if not approval of his mother, she was suddenly terrified to see his reaction. Perhaps he'd think she was slutty like this and she would see nothing but cold contempt in his eyes. Perhaps this was the wrong tactic altogether, she thought in panic. What if it just drove him away? What if she lost him through this stupidity?

Squashing the rising panic, she sat beside him, managing to answer some kind question of Lisa's about the day's boat trip. Beside her, she felt Giancarlo turn his head at last, and when she could avoid it no longer, she faced him. His eyes were on her cleavage, the heavy lids hiding his expression. She felt the heat of embarrassment as well as desire begin to wash through her body, but then his gaze moved suddenly upward and trapped hers.

Not contempt or distaste, but not desire either. *Amusement.*

Bastard, she thought in rage, grasping the opportunity offered by Mario to look away and accept a glass of wine.

Bloody hell! She could lead his brother, Christ, even his

pregnant (as it were) brother-*in-law*, even his damned *father* by the nose, screw any of them stupid before bed-time, they were so lost drooling at her. But he, Giancarlo, who should by any rights already be her lover, *laughed* at her!

Well, then, she'd ignore him. Tonight. Maybe in the morning she could just leave, she thought, heaping her plate with salad. Let him catch Marinuzzi without her.

Abruptly, she turned to offer him the salad bowl, and that very suddenness saved her, for she caught his face before he had the chance to school it. That had been her mistake on arriving. She'd given him too much time to see her, get used to her and work it out before she observed his reaction. The amusement was for her benefit.

But now, in the tiny instant before he took the bowl from her, she saw the overlay of misery in his eyes, the gleam that was pure, unadulterated lust. As he took the bowl, his eyelids closed down, and she knew he wouldn't let her see it again.

If he could help it.

But Via knew her strength now. Deliberately, she let her fingers trail across his hand as she relinquished the bowl, making sure to touch the sensitive area of skin between his thumb and forefinger. Though he gave no other outward sign of agitation, his eyes darted back to hers. She smiled into them, hiding none of the desire she felt. His lip twitched upwards, nervously, before he hastily looked away.

Gotcha!

Happily, Via began to eat. Throughout the meal, she lost no opportunity to let their arms touch, to lean across him to take his and Fabio's plates, so that he got an excellent view down her cleavage. Sometimes he shuddered faintly, though he gave no stronger clue that she was affecting him.

Then, under the disguise of the suddenly animated

conversation going on around them, she turned to him to make some deliberately suggestive comment and found his gaze on her breasts as if glued there. Triumph rose up from her toes, along with a fresh spurt of responsive desire that flooded her thin cotton panties.

Obviously aware of her discovery, he tried to look casually beyond her to his father without meeting her gaze. But there was no time to enjoy his discomfort, or her effect on him, for suddenly her own eye was caught by a movement in the garden.

Somewhere in the shadows of the trees at the far end, near the pathway, someone was lurking.

Marinuzzi.

Her entire body froze. Apart from the fingers of her right hand which suddenly curled round Giancarlo's forearm and gripped like a vise.

Giancarlo moved quickly to stand in front of her, hastily scanning the rest of the garden and the trees.

"What is it?" Lisa asked, half-puzzled, half-amused. Then her gaze fell on Via, and the smile died on her lips before it was properly formed. "Via?"

"She's fine," Giancarlo said quietly, and she knew he spoke to her rather than his sister. "Nothing will happen to her here."

The warmth of his protection melted her paralysis. She breathed again, just as the darkest shadow detached itself from the trees and began to walk toward them with the long, loping stride of a youth who hasn't quite got used to the new length of his legs.

"*Buona sera,*" he called out. To Via's unspeakable relief—after all, she had good reason to know exactly how threatening, how downright dangerous teenage boys could be—he sounded positively awkward. "Didn't mean to startle you," he added as he came closer. "I saw you eating and wondered whether I should come back later."

Giancarlo said, "Roberto."

Roberto? The boy from the café last night.

"Come, sit down, Roberto," Antonia commanded. "What brings you up here tonight? How is your mother?"

"Well, thank you," Roberto said awkwardly. Between his black T-shirt and his blacker hair, his face gleamed oddly white in the light of the terrace lamps. He stood by the table, shifting from one foot to another, but didn't sit, even when Mario pointed to a spare chair near the door that he could pull up. Everyone looked at him expectantly, which seemed to throw him completely.

"I can't stay," he stated. "I need to talk to Giancarlo. In private."

Then, as Antonia frowned at his curt manners, he half turned away. "But I can come back," he muttered.

"No, no." Giancarlo moved round the table toward him. "We'll sit over here."

"What is this all about?" Mario asked Via as they both watched Giancarlo lounge into a garden chair on the smaller terrace farther round the house. He waved Roberto into another on his left, which meant, Via realized, that he could still see her and most of the garden. Again his protection warmed her, even while the chill of its necessity tried to ice her bones.

"I'm not sure."

Frowning, Lisa said, "What did he mean, *nothing will happen to you here*?"

"I suppose, that nothing will."

"Via, is he *working*?" Antonia demanded.

"So far as I know, he's still on sick leave," Via said evasively. "But perhaps the young man has the sort of problem that Giancarlo can help him solve..."

It wasn't a very long conversation, although as the boy effaced himself through the front gate, and Giancarlo resumed his seat next to her, she realized she'd have to wait to find out. With the effortlessness of long practice, Giancarlo fielded all his family's questions, just saying with a casual shrug that Roberto had asked his advice on a private matter.

"If you're working before the doctor permits..." Antonia began.

"Leave it, Antonia, he's not stupid," her husband warned, refilling her glass. "What's for dessert?"

For the first time during that meal, Giancarlo actually exerted himself to be entertaining, distracting his family, no doubt, from their suspicions concerning him and Roberto. Via found no time to question him. Even when she managed to catch his eye and lifted her brow in obvious interrogation, he only smiled faintly.

"I'll get you later," she murmured, rising to the challenge.

Unexpectedly, his smile widened. "No you won't," he said, getting to his feet. "Sorry, people, but I have to sleep. Busy day," he apologized. "Good night."

Antonia looked as though she didn't know whether to be pleased he was taking such care of himself or worried he was so much more tired than last night. Via didn't wait to hear the debate. There was no way he was getting away with that.

Standing without excuse, she ran after him and caught up with him in the doorway.

"Giancarlo," she said, not troubling to lower her voice. "You haven't said goodnight properly."

He turned patiently at her tug on his arm, but he was clearly unprepared for the assault which followed. Wrapping her arms close around his neck, she pushed herself into him and clamped her mouth over his.

She put it all in there, all her anger and frustration as well as her desire, sucking and biting at his lips, sliding her tongue deep into his stunned mouth, probing into every secret corner. At the same time, she moved her body against his so he could feel her thrusting breasts with their hard, anxious peaks.

From semi-erect, his cock stiffened and grew, pushing into her abdomen. She could feel his heart thundering against her breasts, yet he held his body rigid in her arms. Uncaring who saw, she let her arm slide downward, sweeping her hand across his back to the waistband of his shorts, where she delved inside and took hold of his naked buttock.

Giancarlo gasped. His body pressed back, almost involuntarily, she thought. Abruptly, he took control of the kiss, bending her backward with the force. One hand came up to hold her head steady. The other held her bottom so he could push his erection even harder into her. Smiling under his lips, almost sobbing with relief, she allowed herself one moment of the bliss before she tore herself free of both his arms and his mouth.

"Good night, Giancarlo," she said steadily. "What a shame you're too afraid to find out what I'd be like." And she turned on her heel and walked back to the table. She made sure her hips swung, too.

Chapter Ten

Via stood in the arched opening at the top of the tower, trying to let the cool evening air quench her body's fires. She just hoped Giancarlo felt as bad as she did. This was becoming a really stupid game. He'd have to give in soon or they'd both explode!

She let out a gasp of silent laughter. She'd come up here in the hope that he would be there already. He wasn't, and she knew now he wouldn't come, not tonight. So, with the salty taste of sea air on her lips and the peaceful shushing of the waves drifting across the town and through the window, she tried to calm herself enough to sleep. Despite the massive satisfaction he'd given her earlier, she was in desperate need of more. Her hand slid down to her anguished crotch and pressed. Time for bed and another date with her own fingers.

She turned from the view that never seemed to receive its proper due from her, and froze.

Footsteps were running lightly up the spiral stairs. Via drew in her breath. *Him.* She knew his step...

He paused halfway up, and Via heard his soft knock.

"Via?"

Forcing herself, Via strolled across the open tower room to the door. By the time she set her foot on the stair, he'd opened the bedroom door and peered inside.

"Looking for me?" she enquired, while her heart beat so fast it seemed to rock her whole body.

"Yes, come down."

Laughter caught in her throat. "So forceful," she mocked, brushing past him into the room. "Maybe I'm not available tonight, Giancarlo."

"I don't want you to be available," he said grimly, closing the door and leaning against it. "I want you to be careful."

"I'm *ultra*-careful—pill *and* condoms."

His head leaned back against the door, and she realized with a first stab of guilt that he was actually deathly tired. Fear twisted through her, silencing her unruly tongue.

"Can we stop the sexual games, Via? Just for a moment?"

"You started them." She couldn't resist that. "But I'm more than willing to give them up."

"Good." His gaze came back to her. "I'm going out now. I want you to lock the door when I've gone." Brushing past her, he reached up to close the window and snib it. Via watched him uncomprehendingly. The chill she associated with Marinuzzi began to climb once more.

"Why? Where are you going?" she demanded in panic. "What did Roberto tell you? Is Marinuzzi up to his tricks here?"

He hesitated. Then, turning to face her, he said, "Yes, I think so. Roberto is involved with some local Satanist cult. It started as kids on their own, trying, or pretending to try, to raise the Devil, but last year, Marinuzzi's boys joined in and it got a little more serious. Now they follow Marinuzzi Senior, animals are killed, people are hurt, their own people so far and none of it fatal. Silly girls being cut for ritual blood-letting and too frightened either to object, report it or get out. Roberto wants out. He asked my advice on how to do it, and to stop

Marinuzzi at the same time.

"Tonight and tomorrow night there are meetings scheduled in their Unsacred Place. Marinuzzi summoned them earlier this evening because he'd found the perfect sacrifice."

Via's eyes widened. "Me?"

"I can only suppose so. I'm going to see what they're up to, but you'll be quite safe here. All the doors will be locked, and I've warned Mario and Fabio to stay up on watch until I come back."

Via swallowed, her thoughts and emotions in turmoil. "What if it's a trick?" she said suddenly, as Giancarlo reached behind him to open the door once more. His fingers stilled. She flitted toward him, the words spilling out. "What if Roberto was sent to lure you away? So that you can be killed and I can be captured?"

"No," Giancarlo said with certainty.

"Hell, will you at least consider the possibility?" Via exclaimed, and he smiled faintly.

"I have. But I know Roberto too well. He was quite genuine tonight."

Via bit her upper lip, sweeping one hand through her hair while she thought. Then, lifting her eyes to his once more, she drew a deep breath. "Let me come with you."

"No."

"Please, Giancarlo. We'd have two pairs of eyes to observe with."

"And if you got caught?"

"You can rescue me. And vice-versa," she added with a quick grin.

"This isn't a game."

"Christ, do you imagine *I* don't know that? I have a

personal stake in this! And besides…"

"Besides what?" he demanded. Oddly, it was his impatience that gave her hope. She knew she was getting to him and he hated it.

She smiled lopsidedly. "Besides, for some reason, I feel safer when I'm with you. It doesn't matter where."

A second longer, his dark eyes stared into hers. Then his head fell back once more, knocking against the door with unnecessary force. "Get changed, then. Like that, you're just too…"

"Distracting?" she asked smugly.

"Sacrificial," he growled.

It was the first time she'd worn jeans since the night she'd met Giancarlo. Night was the only time denim was bearable in this country, but in this situation, crawling through undergrowth and sliding up and down hills, they were invaluable.

Giancarlo's car was parked miles away, or so it seemed to Via, scrambling up yet another wooded hill in search of this Unsacred Place that he claimed to know…

"Bull's-eye," Giancarlo said softly over his shoulder. Reaching down, he took her hand and hauled her up beside him to the ridge of the hill. Even through the denim, her knees felt grazed by the thousand tiny, sharp stones hidden in the wild, sun-scorched grass. Below, lit with car headlights as well as flaming torches, was a graveyard. Meandering between the flat and upright stones were familiar hooded figures that made Via feel suddenly sick.

Covering her discomfort, she demanded, "You mean we could have driven all the way here?"

"Oh, yes, if you wanted to join the party."

"Why is there a graveyard here anyway? There's no habitation for miles, is there?"

Giancarlo shrugged. "There used to be a church here, too—I suppose it's deconsecrated ground. The village will have disappeared centuries ago. If we go down the side of this hill, it should bring us close enough to see and hear what they're doing." He glanced at her. "We'll have to cut out the noise, though. Stop talking and mind your feet."

"Yes, boss," she muttered, dragging herself after him.

Fifteen slow and rather painful minutes later, they lay face down among the protective trees, still above the graveyard, but able to peer down into it more closely. It was the chanting that grated on Via. Too similar to what went on the night she'd been kidnapped, the sound of their voices chilled her blood, churned her whole being so she had considerable difficulty concentrating on the scene before her. Gradually, however, the large, calm presence of Giancarlo beside her soothed her fearful memories, and though the chanting accelerated in rhythm, Via's reaction did not. The black-robed dancing figures below, gyrating to the wild beat of their own voices, began to draw together in suggestive, even lewd poses, rubbing against each other until the chanting became more like moaning. From somewhere, some sort of rhythm seemed to be kept, but if there were any words involved now, even ancient or incomprehensible ones, Via couldn't hear them, just the guttural groans and grunts as hands groped and bodies twisted together.

Via saw a couple shimmy down to the ground, had a brief glimpse in the headlights of a white bottom already pumping up and down. Another pair had fallen back against a tree, both pulling up their robes in order to consummate their dance. As they thrust together, Via felt a stirring in her own loins. Half-ashamed, she tried to look away, but just then another hooded figure approached the couple by the tree and, without warning, pulled up his own robe to reveal a pale, stiff cock which he began to rub against the nearest person's ass. The recipient's head flew back in obvious startlement, but he or she—Via couldn't tell the sex of any but the third of the threesome—made no objection.

Via dragged her eyes away, her crotch pressing involuntarily into the hard ground. Shockingly, she was wet. She wanted to jump Giancarlo and to hell with the consequences of discovery.

"What is it?" Giancarlo whispered, presumably catching her quickened breathing.

"Nothing," Via whispered back, her gaze on a girl lying on the ground with a kneeling man thrusting away between her legs. Another man knelt over her face, pushing his cock in and out of her mouth. As she watched, both men obviously came at once, falling into each other's arms while each emptied into the girl beneath them.

Via swallowed, shifting position so that her aching pussy strained against the seam of her jeans. "Funny how much of a turn-on it is from a safe distance," she breathed.

As if he didn't hear, Giancarlo nodded toward a spot immediately below them. "Marinuzzi?" he whispered. Following his gaze, Via saw a hooded figure standing apart from the sexual orgy going on all around him, his face hidden in the shadows of the cowl, but his identity unmistakable. At least to Via. Although this time, it seemed, there was to be no sacrificial victim.

She spoke, or thought, too soon. Abruptly, the hooded figure of Marinuzzi moved and lifted high a tied, squawking cockerel by the feet. And the orgy stopped, almost immediately.

There were a few more demented thrusts and muffled moans, but mostly they pulled themselves apart and approached their leader. It was easier now to see which were women since several of them had at least one breast hanging out of their disordered robes. They all moved with the sort of lethargic swagger associated with the recently aroused and satisfied.

Marinuzzi spoke, intoning something in Latin while he lifted a huge, wicked knife in his hand—Via recognized that, too. It was meant to have murdered her in a ruined chapel in the hills behind Pisa. As easily as if he was cutting bread, Marinuzzi slit the cockerel's throat. Via gasped, unable to prevent it, her fingers finding and digging into Giancarlo's arm. Yet she couldn't look away. Marinuzzi raised the bird, letting its blood drip down his arms and over his face.

Before him, his acolytes had lined up and now came forward one by one and, in a vile parody of the Christian Eucharist, Marinuzzi dripped blood straight from the bird onto their faces. Some actually opened their mouths to receive it.

Christ, hadn't they heard of food poisoning?

When everyone had had their share, they all stood around him expectantly, and he began to speak in normal Italian, for all the world like a priest making his sermon. Via couldn't catch it all, partly because her vastly improved Italian wasn't up to it without being able to read his lips and expression, partly because the distance swallowed up some of the words. But she thought she got the gist of it, which was that the blood of human sacrifice was not only pleasing to Satan, but made his worshippers unimaginably stronger.

"Already I feel the strength, the power of our sacrifices. Especially an empathic virgin who was offered last Walpurgis night. And what I gain, I give to you."

Apart from the two—or is it three?—huge houses, the cars,

the jewelry...

"I will be honest. I need more power to free my sons, to influence stronger and more distant minds, those that cannot be bribed. And the means is walking amongst us, the gifted yet misguided woman who accused my boys in the first place. Tomorrow night, I will bring her to you, make her part of us, give her to Satan that my power—your power!—will grow unimaginably."

His followers gazed at him, apparently rapt. Either that or they didn't give a damn and were just filling in time before the next orgy of sex or blood-letting.

As if he had the same thought, Marinuzzi seemed to scan the crowd. Eventually he raised his arm and crooked one finger. Nothing happened until he repeated the gesture. Then, dragging her feet, a girl edged forward. Someone helped her with a push, no doubt from relief at not being chosen themselves. Again the wicked, silver knife glinted in Marinuzzi's hand.

Giancarlo moved. Glancing at him, Via saw with horror that he held a gun. She'd never seen one up close before and it held a special kind of horror for her, even in this situation. She'd grown up in a country still appalled by the indiscriminate slaughter of children in what should have been a place of safety, and guns were anathema to her. Her mouth opened to forbid him to use it, to persuade, cajole, command. Then she thought of the girl standing in front of Marinuzzi with such terror. She thought of the one who had died last April. Was she the empath he'd spoken of? Had she dreamed this girl's last awful hour? Was that the elusive memory plaguing her since her own capture? It would certainly explain the impossible familiarity of that scene—and of this one.

Her tongue remained clamped between her teeth. Her heart thundered as her gaze flitted between Giancarlo, his gun and the scene below.

And something was definitely happening there. The girl now stood in front of Marinuzzi, staring up at him in perfect silence. Gradually, it seemed to Via, her body relaxed. Her arm lifted slowly. She pushed back her hood and smiled trustfully at the man with the knife. Marinuzzi took her hand and held it out before him. The knife rose.

Giancarlo eased off the safety catch. It didn't even click. Via felt suffocated. She was afraid to breathe.

Marinuzzi slid the knife once across the girl's wrist, then dropped it and lifted the wound to his mouth. The girl's head drifted back in some kind of trance or ecstasy. Even when he let her go, she simply stood there, holding her wrist out in front of her until someone came and dragged her away.

Frowning, Via glanced at Giancarlo. The gun was hidden again. He caught her eye, jerking his head behind them. Understanding, Via backed silently with him. Even as they moved, she could hear the voices starting up again. Marinuzzi seemed to be bidding them farewell until tomorrow night. With their backs against the same tree trunk, Via and Giancarlo waited unmoving while the car doors slammed, the engines started and the voices dispersed. Beams of light from the headlights swept the trees around them and gradually disappeared with the cars.

Apart from the almost-full moon above and the stars winking through the tree branches, it was quite dark. The only sounds Via could hear were her own breathing and the chattering insects.

Giancarlo spoke first. "He's very sure of you. He must know by now you're staying with us—he'll watch the house. We need a trap."

Via cast him a quick look from under her lashes. Vaguely,

she wondered why she wasn't afraid of tomorrow. Giancarlo's strong face, the delicate bones and deep, intense eyes, mesmerized her. She loved the clear outline of his whole head, the powerful slope of his shoulders as he lounged beside her against the tree.

"What do you think?"

Via said, "I think I'm still horny from watching everyone else have sex."

Giancarlo made a noise in his throat. It might have been laughter. Via leaned against him, resting her head on his shoulder while she gazed at his profile.

"What about you, Giancarlo? Weren't you even a little bit turned on?"

He shrugged against her ear. "I didn't think about it," he said loftily. "I was working."

"You're not working now." Lifting her head, she brushed her lips along the rough line of his jaw. He pulled away at once.

"Via, we're staying here for the rest of the night. Make it easy on both of us and back off."

Under her amused stare, he rose to his feet and started getting stuff out of his backpack.

"What if I don't want to make it easy for you? Or for that ramrod you keep in your shorts?"

Hastily he crouched farther over the rucksack, and Via almost laughed. For perhaps the first time in her relationship with him, she felt in control. The thought was intoxicating.

Lazily, she moved, helping him spread the ground sheet. "Can I sleep in your bag?"

"No," he said, throwing a bundle at her. A moment later he flung something smaller and harder. "And you'd better put some of that on as well or you'll be eaten alive."

"Mosquito repellent," she observed, dowsing herself in it. "Is it man repellent, too?"

"I hope so."

Smiling suddenly, Via went and put her arms round him. "Giancarlo, stop being an idiot. Let's just make love."

Because he was crouched, she couldn't get very close, but she could lay her cheek on his. She felt his breath coming in short, quick spasms.

"No way," he said at last. "It works. You stink."

"Bastard," said Via amiably, allowing herself to be pushed gently away.

Via woke with the first light of dawn. Though she wasn't terribly rested, she felt deliciously warm and tingly because she'd lain beside him for hours, pressed as close to him as she could get with two sleeping bags between them. At first, he'd tried pointedly to move away, but when she only followed him, he gave up. So she spooned herself and her sleeping bag around his back and hips—and sleeping bag—and went happily to sleep.

The birds were already singing their forceful morning song. The sun was lightening the sky, getting ready to warm the earth even further. Somewhere close by, a couple of cockerels crowed. Probably, Via reflected, there should have been three of them.

Unwilling to think of that, she opened her eyes to find Giancarlo's sleeping face close by her. For a moment, she just stared at him, letting the rush of pure tenderness wash over her. He looked like a child, almost, innocent and carefree. Almost. His body stirred beside her, and even through the sleeping bag, she felt a pang of lust.

Unexpectedly, his arm threw itself out of its containment

and across her body. Never one to miss a chance, Via snuggled farther in, bringing her lips so close to his that she couldn't resist pushing them closer still until they touched.

His parted invitingly. She knew he was asleep. But it didn't matter, or not enough. She kissed him, gently at first, tasting his full morning lips with sensual languor. He responded, taking over, deepening the kiss until he started to roll over her body.

Every nerve shrieked with joyful anticipation. The butterflies in her stomach danced wildly to the rhythms of her heart. Wetness flooded between her legs, soaking the wispy cotton covering that was all, apart from a T-shirt, that she wore.

His hands were beginning to pull roughly at the sleeping bags in his way, when his eyes flew open into hers. His lips stilled in shock. Hers kept going, sucking on the tongue that was still in her mouth. Hastily, he withdrew it and rolled off her.

"I'm sorry," he said tightly.

"Don't be. I was enjoying it."

He sat up, passing one hand across his shining head. Interestingly, it shook. He glanced back at her. "Did I start that?"

She sighed. "No. I did. But you didn't appear to mind. I think I like you better asleep."

He began to climb out of the sleeping bag. Via let him get so far, drinking in his naked, powerful chest and shoulders, the rippling muscles of his flat stomach and the line of coarse, sexy hair that disappeared into his shorts. Then she crawled out of her own sleeping bag and launched herself into his lap, right on top of his huge, throbbing erection.

Pressing her breasts into his chest, running her hands all over his shoulders and back, she whispered, "Give in, Giancarlo, give in. Neither of us can go on like this." And she fastened her mouth to his once more, this time deliberately provoking him, relying on the fact he was already desperately aroused to ensure that this time he couldn't reject her advances.

Giancarlo tore his mouth free, detached her clinging hands and stood. "Leave me alone, Via," he warned.

"Or what?" she taunted, partly to cover her hurt, the flagging of her confidence that he truly wanted her and would take her in the end. He began to roll up his sleeping bag with short, abrupt movements. Watching him, Via repeated, "Or what, Giancarlo? You'll have to have some fun? A little sex, a little love with someone you actually want? Or do you just lack the courage to tell me you don't fancy me anymore?"

On the last word she stood, turning her back and walking deliberately to her sleeping bag, which had got swept a couple of feet farther off when she'd launched herself at him. Wearing only the sexy, black lace knickers and the skimpy top, she made sure her hips swung as she moved, and she knew he watched her. She could feel his glare burning into her skin.

Good. Watch and weep!

Bending from the hips, she picked up her sleeping bag. But before she could even straighten, she heard him move behind her. He hit her like a cannon ball, just as she stood erect, before she could even turn to face him, and the force of it pushed her against the nearby tree. With a gasp of excitement, she felt his erection pressing into the soft flesh of her bottom.

"Is this what you want?" he demanded breathlessly in her ear. "Is this what you're plaguing me for? You want me to fuck you hard up against this tree, like you saw those randy kids doing last night?"

His breath was hot on one cheek. The other pressed into the rough bark of the tree. Casting her eyes up until she could see his own blazing down at her, she felt a jolt of something that was not fear and yet was more than excitement or desire. His hips pushed harder, forcing her crotch against the tree, grazing the soft skin of her thigh. She didn't care. Lust raged through her.

Twisting so she could reach his lips, she breathed, "Yes..." before flickering her tongue across them. He laughed, a harsh, ragged sound, and she felt his hand delve around the curve of her hip and thigh, forcing itself between her legs until his fingers touched her pussy. She heard his groan through her own gasp of shooting sensation.

"My God, you do, too. You're so wet I could bathe in you." His teeth bit her lips, slid across her jaw line to her nape, sucking.

Via gasped, twisting with pleasure. The fingers on her pussy deftly slid aside the drenched cotton, then left her. She cried out in distress.

"Oh, don't worry," he ground out. There was some twisting behind her, some rustling, and she realized with desperate anticipation that he was rolling on a condom. "This time, I'll finish it." And she cried out again as he pushed his cock right inside her.

It was huge, filling her, but he gave her little time to get used to his size. He thrust all the way in so that his body held her jammed up against the tree. She gasped at the feel of him inside, a sort of exquisite agony, but already he was pulling back for another thrust which came quickly, making her moan out loud as thrills shuddered through to every nerve ending, wildly pleasurable, like nothing that had ever come before.

"Again?" he whispered in her ear. "You want more like this?"

"More," she gasped. "Oh, yes, more!"

He hammered her, pounding her into the tree. At the same time, his hands slid around, pushing up the T-shirt so he could hold and knead her breasts, flicking his thumbs roughly across the hard nipples. Then they swept down her sides to hold her hips steady for his fucking.

It was a wild coupling, begun with almost as much anger as desire on his part. Yet Via could do little but welcome his furious caresses, thrusting her bottom back into him, twisting and writhing on his cock, her every pleasure obvious in her continuous cries and moans. She felt the change in him, knew he kept the pace because it pleased her and because there was nothing else he could do now he'd started it on such a level. The tree bark grazed her breasts, pressed into her nipples, her stomach, her crotch as he thrust into her, and she gloried in every sensation, reaching greedily for her climax, which came all too quickly.

Feeling the contraction begin, he muttered something unintelligible, turning her face up with one hand so he could watch her as she came, his blazing eyes avidly devouring her. She hid nothing from him, screaming out the stunning joy that hit her so violently, sweeping her away and keeping her there while still he pounded her. At last he took her hands, wrapping her arms under his around the tree, resting his face on the bark above her as if to hide it as he fell into his own joy.

She felt it, though. He didn't cry out with the abandonment she had, but he couldn't stay completely silent either. Muffled groans and tortured gasps told their own story as his body shook and shuddered wildly over hers, inside hers.

When eventually it calmed to a mere trembling of the legs—and she didn't know which of them shook the most—she slid her fingers up his arm to his hidden face.

"What's this?" she teased unsteadily. "Did you think I

wouldn't know you'd come?"

His ferocity, the brutality of his lovemaking, hadn't frightened her at all, yet now it was over, she was afraid, terribly afraid, of his withdrawal. If he tried to pretend this had never happened, that this astounding sex between them meant nothing...

She couldn't see his face, but her fingers could feel his smile. The relief nearly brought her to her knees, except that the weight of his body held her up.

"That's it," he said. "I thought you wouldn't know."

He lifted his head, sliding out of her very, very slowly.

"Jesus," Via whispered, closing her eyes as her pussy began to tingle meaningfully once more. Giancarlo turned her in his arms and held her against his chest. Only when her eyes opened, gazing into his still hot, clouded ones, did he lower his head and kiss her mouth deeply, consumingly.

At last, purely from lack of breath, the kiss broke. Via laid her cheek against his naked chest, sweat-damp in the cool of morning. His arms tightened around her and then he let her go. Bending, he picked up her sleeping bag.

"Time to go back," Via sighed. Between her legs lurked stinging fire and contentment.

"No," said Giancarlo. Under her bewildered observation, he shook out the sleeping bag and spread it on the ground sheet. He glanced at her, and the look in his eyes was enough to set her heart lurching and her stomach spinning downward. "Time to do it again, a little more slowly."

Chapter Eleven

In fact, it was a lot more slowly. This time he took off the rest of her clothes and his and used those big, clever hands to arouse her, exploring and caressing her body in places she'd forgotten she had. Lying naked beneath him, she allowed him the control he seemed to need, and truly there was little hardship in having her body pleasured so thoroughly, aroused to a peak she hadn't believed possible before he finally gave her release. Even then he made her come on his fingers, and then for his mouth, before he finally entered her again.

Understanding her soreness from their previous, savage encounter, he was incomparably tender, his movement within her slow and sensual, with none of the frenetic pounding of the last time. And yet, although she hadn't believed she could reach any pleasure half as great as that first unexpected explosion of passion, the sweetness rose with shattering intensity. His fingers stroked her clitoris, his lips teased her breasts, his tongue snaked over the tight, hard nipples until she cried out her unstoppable joy. As her body arched into him, convulsing in orgasm, he buried his mouth in hers and cried out his own massive release into her throat. Curiously, his shout seemed to vibrate and echo inside her, reigniting her fading fire, setting her over the edge yet again.

"Wow," she said when she could finally speak. Reaching to

touch his face with her fingers, she smiled a little tremulously. "I have to say, Giancarlo, that you are worth waiting for."

"I meant to be, God help me." Lowering his body, he slid out of her so he could lie on his side, still breathing heavily. His fingers traced the line of her lips, then he leaned closer and kissed them. He whispered, "You're the sweetest lover I've ever known. I knew you would be..."

Already basking in his loving, she began to glow at his praise. "I don't have to be sweet," she pointed out.

His eyes gleamed. "I'd like to explore the alternatives some time."

"Me, too," she whispered.

"Tsk tsk, what would all those strait-laced brothers of yours say?"

"What?" Via stared at him.

He blinked. "I didn't say anything."

In one jerk, Via sprang onto her knees and glared wildly around the trees.

"Screwing the policeman? Really! Did you think that would save you from me? On the contrary, my dear, it merely prepares you, though I'm glad you had such a good time."

In terror, Via threw herself into her anxious lover's arms. "He's in my head, Giancarlo! He's in my head!"

Giancarlo was extremely worried. Driving home, he glanced frequently at Via's stiff profile beside him. She had turned so quickly from purring, contented sex kitten to terrified child that he felt somewhat at a loss.

A down-to-earth man, he had great difficulty believing in anything he could not see, hear or touch. Although he had dealt with Satanic ritual crime before, he'd regarded the perpetrators as dangerously misguided fools, or violent sadists looking for an excuse. The idea that anything concrete could actually be achieved through devil worship was anathema to him.

And yet Via believed it. Via believed Marinuzzi was achieving powers and constantly enhancing them through the blood of his victims.

"That girl was dead for three months," Giancarlo reminded her. "Marinuzzi never spoke to you telepathically all the time you stayed with him, not even the night of your kidnapping. What you're hearing now could be the result of your trauma. You know you recovered from that very quickly, maybe too quickly."

"Because of you," she said at once. Giancarlo's heart twisted at that. He liked to hear her say such things far more than he would ever admit, and yet he was both uncomfortable and frustrated that she wouldn't consider a rational alternative to her own theory. She glanced at him now, hesitation in her rather lovely green eyes.

Giancarlo felt a quick stirring in his loins. Sex with Via had been amazing. Somehow she managed to combine sweetness with fierce passion, a delicious surrender with joyful eagerness, and the memory of her soft flesh writhing ecstatically under him was not one he was likely to forget. Despite the stupendous pleasure he'd enjoyed with her, he was already keen to have her again.

Hastily, he turned his gaze back to the road.

Via took a deep breath. "Maybe this is *all* to do with you. The last time, in Manarola, was different. I think you were right then, that I picked up his thoughts without him being aware of it, let alone sending them to me. But this time, he was *there*, and he knew what we'd just done."

"Peeping pervert," Giancarlo said as lightly as he could. But

Via was vehement.

"Exactly! Inside my head, sneaking, stealing. That's what I feel..."

"You weren't feeling it at the time, as I recall," Giancarlo pointed out, earning himself a look of impatience.

"No, I was too taken up with you. I had no time or space or inclination to deal with anything else. It was all pretty...intense."

"I remember."

At least that won him a fleeting smile. She seemed to calm a little. Then, just when he began to hope he might get through to her with a few careful words, she said in a small, determined voice, "I think I—we—changed something, inside me, by doing what we did. Marinuzzi was so strong, so clear this time..."

Oh, Jesus Christ! "You mean sex has given you ESP?" Giancarlo mocked blatantly now, determined to make her snap out of it.

"Enhanced it," Via corrected. She didn't even seem to notice his attitude. Her mind was quite elsewhere.

"Oh come off it, Via!" he exclaimed. "You were hardly a virgin."

No sooner were the words out of his mouth than the idea hit him with all the staggering force of a club on the back of the head.

I have to say, Giancarlo, that you are worth waiting for.

He turned to her, staring.

"Were you?"

She gazed straight ahead as if concentrating on something else, and yet he knew she'd heard every word. A faint flush rose into her cheeks.

"I don't think that's important," she said at last. "I think it was the joy." As if plucking up the courage, she turned to him. While anxiety and guilt and delight all washed over him in powerful confusion, Giancarlo kept his eyes on the road. She said, "I've never known such joy before."

If he hadn't been driving he would have closed his eyes at the pain of that. As it was, he threw his head back against the seat rest. "Because you've never known anyone else." He looked at her. "That's the truth, isn't it? Somehow you've managed to keep that incredible body *virgina intacta*. How old are you?"

"Twenty-eight."

"How? Why? You can't tell me you've been short of admirers. Did none of them do it for you? Why the hell did you pick on me?"

Her face was fiery red now, and not from the heat of the sun beating in her side window. "I...I keep myself distant from people. If you want the truth, I'm afraid of their laughter, their scorn because...because of the way I am. I'm *not* stupid, despite what everyone thought at school, and I don't want to be *thought* stupid by my intellectual equals. Or inferiors."

"You don't need to compare intellects to go to bed," Giancarlo observed.

"I do." Her voice was so small he glanced at her, but again she wouldn't meet his gaze. "I can't pick up strangers. I can't *touch* strangers. I usually avoid the men who attract me—fear of rejection, I suppose—and they're generally spoken for, anyhow. And then, the older I get, the more men expect me to know, the less confident I feel..."

Giancarlo pulled onto the side of the road. A red sports car whizzed past with a blare of the horn that he barely heard. He didn't even trouble with the normal rude gesture. One hand gripping the wheel so hard his knuckles shone white, he tuned to gaze at her.

"Why me?" he repeated.

She sat with her head bowed, staring at her hands. Her fingers were twisting together, over and over until, as if she sensed his scrutiny, she deliberately stilled them.

Her silence made him angry again, fueling his guilt. "Curiosity finally got the better of you?"

"No!" Her head jerked up as though he'd stung her. Her eyes flashed into his. "You know it wasn't like that!"

"Then what?"

"I don't know. What attracts anybody to anybody else? You were kind to me. I liked you. There was *something* about you—I don't know. I liked the way your eyes smiled. I liked your body, and I wanted you. And I liked that you wanted me. You didn't seem to judge me, just accepted me, warts—bruises—and all."

Her eyes bored into his, stormy and miserable. Her voice shook. "But you're judging me now, aren't you, Giancarlo? You're punishing me because you were the first. A hundred years ago, I'd have been cast off for *not* being a virgin. Why are women always to blame? I'm getting out here. When you make it home, send me a bloody taxi!"

He had to move quickly as she wrenched open the door and flung herself away from him. Reaching across, he seized her by the shoulders and slammed the door shut again. She struggled against him, pulling away so he had to hold her very tightly to bury his face in her hair.

"Sh-sh," he whispered. "Don't, Via, I'm sorry... I'm not blaming you for anything. How could I? I'm angry with myself, I'm blaming *myself.* It never entered my head that I would be the first. I should never have been so rough. I'm..."

"Don't you dare!" Abruptly she stopped struggling, though only to pull his head up so she could glare into his eyes. Her own were wet. "Don't you *dare* apologize for that. Don't take it away from me, don't bloody spoil it!"

"Via!" Helplessly, he brushed at her tears with his fingers. She tried to turn away from him, and when he wouldn't let her, she collapsed onto his chest, gripping his arms with a strength that bruised. "I would never want to hurt you," he got out with difficulty, while the sort of tenderness he'd never known before washed over him and through him. He stroked her hair, noting with detached interest that now it was his own hand which shook.

She said into his shirt, "Did I look hurt?"

An involuntary smile stretched his lips. He buried them in her hair again. "No, I have to say you didn't. You looked more...ecstatic."

A shudder of laughter ran through her body into his. "How do you know? You wouldn't look at me."

"I looked."

"Then stop asking me why." She lifted her head and met his gaze. "Because I don't think you're ready to hear the answer."

"Of course I am. Every man want to know what makes him stand out. Why say yes to me—hell, go after me—rather than the hundred other men who must have asked, or at least beckoned?"

Her fingers dug into his shoulders. He could feel her heart thundering against his chest. She was so adorably rumpled and emotional that he wanted suddenly to take her on the back seat, bring that ecstasy back into her flushed, passionate face...

She drew in her breath. "Because I love you."

He knew the shock must be staring out of his eyes like stalks. Terrified and enchanted, he was completely deprived of the breath to speak, supposing he had any words. He couldn't doubt her sincerity. All he could question was the reality. He was her first. Overwhelmed, she was simply mistaken.

But before he could warn her of her error, she spoke again, tumbling into it. "Don't look so petrified. I'm not proposing marriage. I don't expect any declarations from you at all. You asked, and I answered. It makes no difference, so for God's sake don't turn it into another excuse to push me away."

Involuntary laughter rumbled in his throat. "Oh, Via," he said, resting his forehead against hers. "You will be the death of me."

"That's not my plan," she said, before he could even regret his hasty words. He kissed her mouth.

"When can I make love to you again?"

"Now, if you like," she said at once, and he smiled.

"Even I'm not that big a bastard. Come on, let's go back and get this mess over with."

Since Giancarlo was acting unofficially, he couldn't call on the local Carabinieri for back-up. All he could do—and did—was call in a few favors and ask for a few more from friends. As a result, he had two discreetly armed men in a plain van parked in the street. He had another two in the house for back-up. Then, with Mario and Fabio on watch around the house and garden, he placed himself and Via in the garden as bait and waited.

There was no sign of anybody watching the house. Via herself, much to Giancarlo's relief, said nothing more about Marinuzzi speaking inside her head. He was inclined to believe it'd been a mixture of traumas catching up with her—her kidnap, and the excitement of her first complete sexual experience, combined, no doubt, with a bit of irrational guilt on that subject.

Although she didn't look tense, when he sat close to her, he could feel she was wound up tight as a drum. Once, easing himself into a chair beside her, he said casually, "He won't get you, you know. I won't let him."

She smiled and took off her sunglasses to see him properly. "I know you won't. I always feel safe with you."

"Then what's the matter?"

She shrugged. "Just nervous, I suppose."

He had to ask. Reaching out, he covered her hand with his on the chair arm. "Are you regretting this morning?"

"God, no!"

Which at least was reassuringly fervent. Her words of love this morning still sang in his head, growing in importance and necessity to him... And yet he couldn't shake off the nagging suspicion that what she mistook for love was merely a physical crush, because he was her first lover.

"Can you see them?" Marinuzzi asked into his mobile phone. He sat alone in his big garden in the shade of a palm tree, a glass of freshly squeezed orange juice on a table at his elbow.

"Sure. They're all sitting in the garden, relaxing. The foreign girl and the whole family, apart from Signora Di Ripoli who's inside with some visitors."

"Can they see you?"

"Not unless they train binoculars on the house. I'm at an upstairs window, far enough back not to be obvious."

"Excellent," said Marinuzzi, allowing rare approval into his voice. "I want to know the instant he—Giancarlo Di Ripoli—goes out."

As the afternoon wore on, Via's edginess gradually gave way to boredom, then drowsiness. Closing her eyes, she let her open book fall into her lap and drifted off. After all, it had been an incredible day, the day in which she'd finally made something happen with Giancarlo, something incredibly wonderful. And he'd said she was the sweetest lover he'd known! Beside those things, poor Marinuzzi and his threats simply paled into insignificance. Didn't they?

She basked in the security as well as the excitement of his presence nearby. With her eyes closed, she was aware of him with every other sense she possessed. It made it easy to remember all they'd done that morning, every kiss and caress, every stroke inside her, rough *and* tender and all the gradations in between. She felt her body's soreness with fierce joy, even now longing for a repeat. Tonight, tonight...

As she drifted off, her dreams began with him, confused, erotic dreams that became muddled up with what she'd witnessed in the graveyard. Then the dreams changed. Giancarlo was there, but in uniform now, running full tilt, not to her, but to some other woman—a beautiful, blond woman falling in slow motion to the ground, a tiny red hole in the center of her forehead. Then it was swept away by a furious rush of water that came crashing down from nowhere, sweeping up streets and knocking over houses, no longer the Mediterranean-type stone houses of an Italian city, but flimsy constructions of wood that floated in the water afterward, sometimes with people clinging to them. A baby cried somewhere, but Via couldn't see it. Wildly, a man trawled through the water, and Via knew he was looking for the child. Grief was everywhere, huge, overwhelming tragedy...

"Via!"

Her eyes snapped open. For an instant she fought the clouds of sleep and total disorientation. It was as if the dream still floated behind her eyes, interfering with her vision of reality. "What? What is it?"

"You were dreaming." Gently, Giancarlo reached out and wiped her face with the heel of his hand. Only then did she realize her cheeks, her eyes, were wet with tears. "And not pleasant dreams, I think."

"No," she agreed shakily. "Is he here yet? Do you think he's found somebody better?"

"Marinuzzi? No, and I doubt it. But on the plus side, dinner is ready." A moment longer, he studied her face. "What were you dreaming? All the ills of the world?"

"Yes, I think so," she answered and saw startlement glint briefly in his eyes before he smiled and kissed her. It was a good kiss, tender, only hinting at passion, yet swiftly dispelling the last clouds of the dream.

Via touched his rough cheek.

"That was nice," she whispered when it ended. "Could I have another?"

He smiled, melting her heart all over again. This time, the kiss deepened quickly, feeding her body's arousal. It was just as well his mother came out, talking loudly, demanding the presence of her family at the table. Otherwise, Via felt she would have pushed him over and straddled him.

Instead, parting their lips reluctantly, she rose with him, and they wandered hand in hand toward the table.

As they ate, the *bonhomie* of the men was noticeably forced, at least to Via's observation. Giancarlo was especially restless, waiting with ever-increasing tension for Marinuzzi's move.

Via could have told him not to worry. She knew Marinuzzi wasn't coming. She wasn't sure *how* she knew.

But she did.

Chapter Twelve

Night had fallen. From the bedroom window, Via gazed out at the sea, mesmerized by the glinting of the moonlight on the water. Silence shrouded the house and the dark, shadowy garden, isolating her from her surroundings.

Although she'd been waiting for it, Giancarlo's distinctive knock on her bedroom door made her jump. Spinning round from the window, she found it difficult to breathe, so hard was her heart pounding.

Somehow she made herself walk across the room and throw open the door. And at the sight of him standing there, a dawning smile in his intense brown eyes, the ache between her legs began to throb. Was it really only this morning he'd made love to her for the first time? Moving into the doorway, he put his arm around her waist to draw her inside and close the door. Immediately, her own arms wound themselves around his neck.

"I was so afraid you wouldn't come," she whispered.

His other arm wrapped round her, too, and though he held her loosely, she could feel him hardening against her. Loving it, she pressed closer, lifting her face in open invitation. He kissed her parted lips with a sensual thoroughness that left her weak. And when eventually he lifted his head, she stood on tiptoe and took his mouth back again, as if she couldn't live without it. Her tongue slid along his, entering and exploring his mouth as he did hers. When, his hands in her hair, he deepened the kiss even further, she moaned aloud against his lips and felt them smile as he gently broke it.

"I could spend all night just kissing you," he whispered. The unevenness of his voice thrilled her.

Pressing her hot, wet crotch into his thigh, she said breathlessly, "I challenge you to try."

A hiss of laughter escaped him. He brushed his lips across hers. "I accept. But on another night, not this one. I have to go out."

The disappointment was like a bucket of cold water. And it wasn't much comfort to recognize the rock hardness of his cock now nudging her abdomen.

"Why?" she managed.

"I need to know what Marinuzzi's up to. Don't worry. There are still two Carabinieri outside and another two inside. We've had a shift change, so don't panic because you don't recognize them."

"I don't need them. Marinuzzi won't come now, I know it."

"Good." He kissed the top of her head and let her go. She caught at his arm.

"No, wait, Giancarlo, you don't have to go."

"I do," he protested. "Remember? It's why we're here, to catch Marinuzzi in a crime."

That, she supposed, was indisputable. Yet she was uneasy about Giancarlo going out, and not just because she wanted him in her arms. As he began to detach himself from her hold, she clung harder, digging her fingers into his flesh.

"I'm serious. I know where Marinuzzi is."

He stilled. "Via..."

For an instant it swamped her, the impossibility of

explaining to him the whirlpool of knowledge and understanding that had been galloping on her all day. Especially when it was still so confused in her own head. But she had to try, had to keep him away from the ritual that was already beginning.

"No, you have to listen to me. There's a link between him and me now—I don't like it, but it's there."

"And it tells you what?" He detached her fingers from his arm. "That Marinuzzi's at home having a cup of tea with his wife? That he's suddenly decided to give up all this Satanist nonsense that's already led him to murder at least once?"

"Don't," she pleaded. "This is *real*. I mean, I understand him. He'll find a way that doesn't involve any more risk to himself. He won't risk the local boys being caught kidnapping me again, talking again against his family or even himself. But he knows about you, about us, and I'm so afraid he'll use you, hurt you..." And he was *there*, at the unsacred place. She knew it in her bones. But even if Giancarlo believed her, it wouldn't dissuade him from going.

The closed, impatient look faded from his face. He took her back into his arms, laid his cheek on her head. "I'm a policeman," he reminded her. "I can take care of myself. I promise you, he won't hurt me."

She clutched at his shoulders. "There's more. I know you had mixed feelings about bringing me into this. If you hadn't believed you could keep me completely safe, you wouldn't have done it. I know that. But I'm more than just bait. I can help."

"You *have* helped." He paused, then lifted his head. "He's gathered the kids together again, as we knew he would—and if he can't sacrifice *you*, he's liable to kill someone else. He's almost forced to, having gone to all this trouble, all this build-up. I can't let that happen."

"I know that," she whispered. "But going out there is not the way!"

And yet was there any other option? Had she any right to try and save Giancarlo—from what, she barely understood—when he could prevent murder? But the feeling, the *knowledge* that they should stay away from the ritual was eating her up.

"Can't we work together?" Even to herself, it sounded feeble, and she wasn't surprised he smiled. Clenching her fingers on his shoulders, she shook him. "*Listen* to me! I'm remembering things all the time. The dreams are coming back to me, and I *did* dream about that girl's murder. I heard her thoughts, *I felt her die.*"

His arms tightened convulsively. "Via, that was your own experience, and God knows you were lucky to escape."

"Exactly!" she interrupted. "I don't think it was all one dream, it was like present and future all muddled up. Sometimes I was her, or looking at her—and sometimes it was *me*. That's why my—experience—felt almost familiar, that's why..."

He stroked her hair. "I'm so sorry," he whispered. "I should never have brought you back into all this. We have to talk, but not now."

She drew in her breath, hearing it shudder. "No. *I'm* sorry. It's all spilling out at once and not the way I meant it to. I know you have to prevent him killing anyone, I know we need to catch him, arrest him. But I think...I'm wondering if I can't help with my mind. Maybe I can see things. Oh, don't look at me like that! It was you who first brought up the possibility of my ESP when you asked me to come here."

He nodded a rueful acknowledgment. "Yes. But at the moment it's not mind-power we need. It's police work, and before you ask, no, you can't come with me. Not tonight."

The grim determination in his voice steadied her. His arms fell away, but for a moment longer, he searched her eyes. He said, "If you think of anything, *see* anything that I need to know, call me."

It wasn't all she wanted, but warmth seeped into her heart because he meant it, because he wasn't discounting what she could do. What she might be able to do.

She nodded, touching her forehead to his chest. Then she stepped back.

"Take the cops with you," she suggested, "or at least one of them."

"I'll be fine," he soothed, in the sort of way that clearly stated he would not be taking her advice.

He didn't. A minute later she saw him from the window, walking alone down the garden path and leaving by the front gate. He went in the opposite direction to where the plain white van was still parked. There was nothing Via could do except admire the easy motion of his hips and his tight buttocks in his dark jeans as he disappeared from her view.

An hour later, he still hadn't returned. And Via still stood by the window, slumped against the wall with exhaustion. It was after midnight.

She had to accept that she had no control over this gift she'd discovered. She'd tried to throw out her mind to find a clue to what was happening, to follow Giancarlo, to reach Marinuzzi, to reach anyone. She'd tried to blank her mind and wait for something to come. But nothing did, except the same relentless trickle of self-knowledge and forgotten memories that served only to distract her. It seemed she was incapable of focusing her mind to achieve anything. Fear for Giancarlo kept getting in the way.

At last, Via threw her head back against the wall in frustration. Then she straightened, moved away from the window and began to get ready for bed. After all, she thought, pulling her dress up over her head, she might *dream* something useful. And this time, she might remember.

"Via. It's time."

Desperately, she freed herself of the dress and shot wild glances around the room for the source of the voice. It was more hope than belief. She knew it spoke inside her head, and she knew who it was.

"I hope for his sake you're not asleep."

Her heart jolted. "Whose sake?" she said aloud—and that was worse. Not only did she imagine her voice echoed around the empty house, but it definitely shook.

"Your policeman's, of course."

"Why, what is he to you?" she whispered.

"A means of getting you to come to me." It was the same cold, smooth voice that had offered her wine with her dinner and asked for reports on his sons' progress in English conversation. She'd never cared for it. It was the voice of an actor playing a superior role, but now it chilled her from the inside out. And not just because it talked of Giancarlo. Fear made her fight back.

"There are no means of getting me to come to you, arsehole!"

"Tsk tsk. Giancarlo hopes you are wrong. So do I. I really don't want to kill a Carabinieri officer at this stage, but if I have to, I will."

"You couldn't kill Giancarlo. You couldn't get *near* him."

"My dear child, I am *near him. Very near. Near enough to kick, since he lies here at my feet, immobilized, you might say."*

"You're lying," Via whispered, both trembling hands held to her head, wishing she were as mad as Giancarlo had thought this morning.

Marinuzzi's laughter filled her head, dropping her to her knees.

"Get in his car and drive to the graveyard you overlooked last night."

"Is that where you are? Where *he* is?" she whispered, struggling to keep the hope out of her voice now.

"Of course it is. And where you'd better be within the hour unless you want him dead. But don't be silly, Via—you have to come alone. Without either escort or following, or I'll kill him anyway."

"But I can't drive."

There was a faint pause. When he spoke next, he sounded uncertain for the first time. *"Don't be ridiculous. Everyone can drive."*

"No, they can't. And I couldn't even direct anyone there, because I have no sense of direction. Literally. I'm severely dyslexic. I can't find my way out of the house without a bloody guide!"

Her panic now was quite genuine. She tugged at her hair in her anxiety and frustration, striding round and round the little bedroom in her underwear as if movement could relieve the awfulness of losing him through her own fearful inadequacy. For a few hours she'd begun to believe she had some special gift that could more than make up for her shortcomings. She'd dreamed the murder, she'd dreamed her own ordeal. She couldn't deny the gift, but what the hell *use* was it if it couldn't save the man she loved?

"You'd better be lying," said Marinuzzi coldly.

"I'm not lying," she whispered. "Ask Giancarlo. Wait, let me bring his brother. He's bound to know the way if Gian—"

"No."

"Then what do you want?" she demanded. "How can I get to him? Take a taxi?"

"If necessary."

Yanking open the wardrobe door, Via reached for her jeans. Only when she caught sight of herself in the mirror, pulling them onto her legs, did the idea come to her. It was mad and dangerous, probably stupidly so, yet...

She fastened them, then grabbed a T-shirt. "Marinuzzi, are you still there?"

"Of course."

"Can you see what I'm doing? Through my eyes?"

There was a pause, then: *"Interesting idea. I think you'd have to let me."*

And if she did, would she ever get him out of her head again? Could she live with a perpetual snoop?

Could she live without Giancarlo?

Via closed her eyes, trying to concentrate on the voice in her head, instinctively homing in on its distinctive frequency, its unique *feel* within her mind. In the circumstances, it wasn't difficult. Then, opening her eyes, she gazed intently at her reflection in the mirror. "Can you see that?"

"I can see you... Interesting!" He actually sounded excited.

"All right. If I can make the car go without crashing it, can you tell me how to get to you?"

"I think so, yes. Clever girl. I shall enjoy adding your—gifts—to my own."

"One thing, Marinuzzi," Via said, striding across to the

window and opening it. "If you've harmed Giancarlo, I swear I'll kill myself before you get me anywhere near your stupid ritual." She meant it, too. Without Giancarlo, she realized, she didn't want to live. The knowledge made her want to weep, except there was no time for such nonsense.

"Fair point. Just get here. And remember, if you're followed, he dies."

It was the weirdest journey of her life. It began by climbing down the wisteria that wound all around the villa's walls, scattering avalanches of the beautiful purple petals like uncontrollable dandruff, and continued with her stealing Giancarlo's car.

By the time she all but fell down the last few feet into the well-tended earth, her arms ached and her nerves were stretched to screaming point in case she was seen. She climbed from the open window at the top of the tower to avoid observation from the white van, but it made for a longer climb and she was no longer twelve years old, escaping from her brothers' protective custody.

As she clambered to her feet, wiping earth off her face with the back of her hand, a sudden burst of laughter sent her scurrying back against the wall, trying to lose herself among the wisteria. It took a moment to realize the sounds were coming from inside the house. She took a deep breath, trying to slow the drumming of her heart, and began to creep around the house toward the driveway.

Night had turned the pleasant garden into a place of menace, where every dark shadow was a threat. Despite the alien presence in her head—she couldn't forget Marinuzzi for an instant—Via had never felt so alone in her life. Because even the good guys—Fabio, Mario, Giancarlo's friendly policemen—

were now a danger to her and Giancarlo.

At the corner of the house, she paused, trying to accustom her eyes to the dark as she gazed toward Giancarlo's car in the driveway and, in the street beyond it, the white van. But time was short, and Marinuzzi loomed ominously in her mind. She dropped and crawled on her belly toward the driveway.

With each advance she expected a warning call from the window. Every hair on the back of her neck stood up in awareness. She wondered if she'd even hear the shout over the thundering of her heart.

Finally reaching the driver's door, she knelt in the protective shadow of the car to ease open the unlocked door, and slid silently into the seat.

Her hope was that the police observers would assume it was Giancarlo himself and leave her alone. She needed that and a lot of other luck if she was to survive this journey and free Giancarlo.

But in this case, her obsession with Giancarlo stood her in good stead. She knew the sign by which he identified himself to the police, because she'd watched him do it only this afternoon.

And she knew how to start a car. She'd seen it often enough. A swift scan of the dashboard and she was as ready as she could be. The key'd been left thoughtfully in the ignition, no doubt in preparation for the car chase Giancarlo had expected earlier, so she reached with one trembling hand and turned it. As soon as the motor surged to life, she pressed the button for the windscreen wipers, let the wipers make two strokes, then switched them off. *Please God, let it be enough...*

She had a spot of trouble distinguishing between the pedals, but Marinuzzi helped her out there, making her jump with his impatient instructions in her head. After that, it was easy enough to guide the car onto the road. She didn't pause to close the gates behind her, but sped off downhill, away from the white van, praying no one could see her outline in the darkness. Even with her hair flattened against her head she couldn't kid herself she looked anything like Giancarlo.

Despite her frequent checks in the rear view mirror, there was no sign of the van or any other vehicle following. It seemed she'd got away with it. But it was only the first challenge.

With Marinuzzi's voice in her head telling her when to change gears, she drove where he told her. Fortunately, the roads were quiet, so her poor distance judgment didn't matter too much. Just once she took a perverse but savage delight in startling Marinuzzi from his complacency by veering far too close to an oncoming truck. Despite everything, she first felt a fierce enjoyment of this new power. To be able to control a car, to drive *herself* along long, winding roads... Roads that made her think with dissatisfaction of her own meandering life. Without purpose, until now.

As she drove, she discovered, too, that she could communicate silently with Marinuzzi. But she had to be careful here. There was such a fine line between what she projected and what he could trawl from her mind. How to think, *left or right*? to him, while wildly planning, for her own head entirely, how to get herself and Giancarlo out of this?

Once he said tauntingly, "*You see what power you could have had with the right master?*"

"Correct me if I'm wrong," she muttered. "I thought the power was mine."

"Oh, you have great latent power," he allowed. *"It just needs to be focused. Think what you could achieve with it!"*

"You mean I could become an arsehole like you?"

"An arsehole with the ability to influence the rich and the powerful, to gain wealth, political and social power, if such is

your wish, the man you desire, health...?"

"You can do that?" The words tumbled from her mind unbidden this time. Hastily, she clamped down on it.

"Of course. Wouldn't you have liked that gift to give your sick policeman?"

"He's not sick."

"Yes, he is. Everyone knows he has cancer."

"*Had* cancer. He's clear of it now."

"Is he? Wouldn't you like to be sure? Wouldn't he?"

"Why are you asking me this? I'm going to die, remember?"

"Call it a reward. If you give me no trouble, I'll cure your policeman by way of thanks."

Via said nothing. Holding her mind shut, she dashed the tears out of her face so she could see out of the windscreen. To give Giancarlo the gift of life with her death...? Emotion swamped her, battering her.

From such a source, would he want this gift? Was it truly hers to give? He need never know. He just needed to live. *She* needed him to live, with or without her.

In her mind, Marinuzzi laughed. *"Thinking about it? Tempted? Well, consider it when you judge me. Everyone has their price. Would you not truly worship Satan if he would bring life and health to your lover?"*

"Crossroads," Via snapped. "Which way?"

He brought her to a halt in a different place from the one they'd left the car in the last time. And when she slowly took the keys out of the ignition and opened the car door, she could hear the voices already, see the glare of headlights. Via climbed out, glancing up at the looming black hills behind. Yes, surely that was where she and Giancarlo had been last night, looking down on this.

There was the graveyard, bathed in light. There were the black-hooded figures, swaying, chanting—no sex tonight, or not yet. Perhaps they'd got all that over with while waiting for her. Via's throat closed up with fear.

As one cowled figure detached itself from the shadows and came toward her, she could control the terror only by thinking of Giancarlo. By coming here, she'd freed him. And somehow she knew that, with him free, she would be all right, too, in the end. She kept that vision of him before her eyes: Giancarlo when she'd barely met him, big and calm and solid, moving inexorably out of the shadows to stand beside her in the hotel carpark where the youths had threatened her.

"Interesting mode of travel," said the figure approaching her. He sounded amused.

Via wasn't. In sudden fury, she threw him out of her head, closing all access. She wasn't sure how. It was simply instinct. She could feel him beating on her mind to get back in, like a moth's wings on a window pane.

"Get out of my head, you bastard," she said between her teeth, too angry to be either triumphant or surprised by her success in keeping him out. "Where is Giancarlo?"

The cowled figure paused before her. He reached up one hand and pushed back his hood. He was smiling, the pale headlight glow glinting on his teeth like a surreal toothpaste advert.

"Really," said Marinuzzi, "I haven't the foggiest idea."

The blood pounded in her head, sang so loudly in her ears that she thought she would go deaf or faint. Or both.

Oh, Jesus Christ, let me be wrong...

Aloud, she stammered, "What do you mean? What have you done with him?"

Marinuzzi's smile broadened. "Nothing. Nothing at all. I haven't laid eyes on him since our fortuitous meeting in Manarola."

Via closed her eyes. When she opened them, there were hooded figures on either side of her, seizing her arms to prevent her retreat.

"It's sweet really," Marinuzzi marveled. "Still so trusting."

Oh, Giancarlo, what have I done?

All the horror was seeping back. With the weird sense of déjà vu that had been with her all her life, she felt them pull her across to the big upside-down cross they'd nailed to a tree and push her against it. And, though she knew she was just doing what she'd done so pointlessly before, she struggled, lashing out with her knees and feet, twisting her arms and her body in their hold until someone hit her in the face hard enough to make her dizzy. After that, somebody obviously decided there were too many cooks spoiling this broth, because a large, impatient person abruptly pushed his fellows out of the way and pinned her to the cross with his body while he efficiently bound her hands behind it.

Almost more appalling than all the rest, she could feel his semi-arousal against her body and, instead of being revolted, she found herself remembering Giancarlo's body against her, pushing into her. Giancarlo, whom she would never see again, unless she could somehow...

But her hands were tied. The big lad holding her moved aside, and she saw the other dark, hooded figures gathering like crows around a dropped sandwich in winter, advancing on her. Inevitably, fresh panic drove her to tug fiercely, futilely at her bonds. The lad who'd tied them glanced behind her as if to make sure they were holding, and that was when she realized that, though the rope felt firm enough, it was hardly tight. And her feet were free.

Had the boy felt sorry for her? Her heart lurched with unexpected hope. Was it Roberto? The boy who'd told Giancarlo of this meeting place? Via couldn't remember him being so tall, but then she'd never been standing at the same time as him before. Either way, surely there was a tiny chance of escape now, if she could just wriggle free and run as she had done before.

Except Giancarlo believed she was home in bed. He was highly unlikely to drive by in a friend's taxi this time! Unless he went to her room when he came home. Perhaps he already knew she'd gone and was looking for her. Or was he here already, watching from the same vantage point as last night? Would he know her over this distance? And did it matter? Whether he could recognize her or not, he would shoot whoever tried to hurt her. Even if it was one of these stupid, misled kids.

Oh God, how did it come to this? How do I live with causing death? If I live at all...

Forcing herself to alertness, Via took stock of her surroundings. Only the tall boy—surely Roberto—remained beside her, his fellows having slunk away as if to be as distant as possible when the deed was done. In front of her stood Marinuzzi himself, hood still down, leading the chanting of some new, incomprehensible incantation. Even as she watched him, he raised aloft the big, silver knife she'd seen before, and her blood froze again.

Of course, he was in a hurry. Not only had she managed to escape him the last time, but he was probably aware that Giancarlo and the police knew of this place. His plan depended on Giancarlo's own: guarding her at home, baiting Marinuzzi to come to him. But he had to do it quickly.

Well, perhaps she was at least to be spared the ritual rape. Was that really all she had left to hope?

The cockerel was brought to him, its beak and legs bound. Via closed her eyes as he drew the knife across its throat. An instant later, a rustling movement warned her to open them again, yet before she could, a stream of warm liquid hit her head, running down her forehead into her face, clogging her eyes, seeping into her mouth.

Via yanked at her bonds, threw her head from side to side, her mouth opening in an uncontrollable gasp. Mistake. She tasted blood, sour and salty and rank.

"Oh, Jesus, Jesus!" she cried out in as much disgust as despair. And for the first time in years, she also uttered the name in quite unconscious prayer. She only realized the last, numbly, when Marinuzzi suddenly struck her across the mouth, hissing something at her in contemptuous, angry Italian. She had no time to work it out. Already he'd turned away from her, lifting the knife high, both hands raised to the sky. Words, strange, alien-sounding words spilled from his lips. Before Via's bemused eyes, his fingers seemed to crackle with some sort of electricity.

She would have thought she imagined that had not the hooded acolytes stepped back, as if in awe, or even terror. Their chanting all but ceased. What was left was somehow pitiful, trailing off into nothing as Marinuzzi's suddenly huge voice filled the graveyard. Only it no longer sounded like Marinuzzi. It had deepened, expanded until it echoed, until it sounded like some mythical beast speaking from his mouth. She could almost *see* it, a shadow of horns and snarling lips around long, dripping teeth.

Primal fear paralyzed Via. The last time she'd been held like this, she'd been afraid of human beings, of what other people were prepared to do to her. This time, it was more basic, a primeval, all-encompassing terror of the unknown, of spirits she hadn't known she believed in and powers she'd never thought to witness.

And it was that power which was going to kill her. Marinuzzi would wield the knife any second, and she wouldn't be able to move, because no earthly power could withstand what he'd called down now. What he would become. Even Giancarlo couldn't save her. It was too late for that.

All she could do was pray.

She began in a silent, fervent whisper, the Lord's Prayer tumbling from lips that barely moved, though the words shouted in her head. Over the last couple of hours it'd all got so confused, what was thought and what was spoken, so she had no idea whether the voice she heard rising with Marinuzzi's was outside or inside her head. She just knew it was hers.

"Hallowed be thy name! Thy Kingdom come! Thy will be done!" In her mind, she was louder than he. *Then let him know, let him hear!* Lifting her head now, she roared with her mind as well as her voice, hurling the words at the transfixed acolytes.

"On Earth as it is in Heaven! Give us this day our daily bread!"

To one side of her, she became aware of Marinuzzi also shouting, snarling, his arms still raised above his head. Forks of lightning passed between him and the blackened sky, though Via couldn't tell in which direction. The flash of light seemed to cast some grotesque shadow across his face, transforming it for an instant into the beast she'd imagined earlier. Some tiny part of her froze with fear inside. Outside, like some hysterical witch, she continued to yell out her defiance, her fight, in the only prayer she could remember. And for some reason, some blind, foolish reason, she felt as if she was winning. The kids before her seemed more terrified of her than of Marinuzzi, and her own voice was the one she could hear above all other sounds.

Maybe Marinuzzi felt it, too, for when he turned his head finally to look at her, his face was contorted in hatred, a pure hatred quite free of the urbane humor he'd used in his callous dealings with her before. Uncaring now because she knew he would kill her, her only muddled, hazy aim was somehow to make him end it with that, to deprive him of power or followers or both. She glared into his face and, although he'd fallen silent, she yelled on, "For Thine is the kingdom, the power and the glory, forever and ever!"

Through it all, she heard him hiss in Italian, "Die now, little trollop. I'll still have your powers to use, I'll still win!"

The great silver knife glinted in the white light of the moon as he swept it down with force. This time, she refused to close her eyes. She knew they were pouring with tears, for her family and for Giancarlo, for a life that wouldn't now be, yet she wouldn't stop praying, bellowing the words to the world as well as to God.

And abruptly, like an answer to her pleas, Marinuzzi stumbled backward, as if an invisible hand had shoved him.

It wasn't invisible, of course. It had just moved very fast. And it did so again. Roberto, the tall boy at her side, swung in front of her, uncaring of the wicked knife in Marinuzzi's hands. His arm, his fist, flew, and Marinuzzi dropped like a stone.

Via stared. She couldn't stop praying, but she stumbled over the words now, cried over them. Before Marinuzzi even hit the ground, Roberto had the knife in his own hands and launched himself at her.

She knew an instant of renewed fear, that Roberto was after the power for himself, but then he was behind her, slitting the ropes that bound her hands. How had she forgotten about the ropes, about escape? All she'd been doing was praying, praying, "Our Father, who art in Heaven..."

"Stop, Via, stop, it's over," Roberto whispered, catching her as she tumbled forward and gathering her into his arms. Achingly, he sounded like Giancarlo, he *felt* like Giancarlo.

Dimly, she became aware of other noise, of shouting, screaming, a stampede of running, pounding feet, whistles blowing.

"The police are here," Roberto said. "Hush now." And he still sounded like Giancarlo.

With an immense effort, Via forced her lips to silence. A gurgle came from her throat and then it was silent, too, while she peered inside the cowl. He pushed it back off his smooth head, and she gazed into the face of Giancarlo.

A huge racking sob rose up from her toes and choked her. Collapsing against him, she howled out her terror and pain for this world and the next. And her joy. And her love.

Chapter Thirteen

He'd been there all along. Having left her in her bedroom, he collected Roberto and drove to the graveyard on his motorbike. He wore Roberto's spare robes (apparently a girl in the group made them for everyone—Via laughed weakly at that) and actually saw her arrive. Notifying the police via his mobile phone, he joined the throng in order to give her some protection until the cavalry came, which it did, in fact, only after he'd been obliged to hit Marinuzzi.

"I'm so sorry I let that happen to you," he whispered into her hair as he held her tightly in the back of a police car. "But until the sparks flew, until you started singing..."

"Praying," Via corrected. "I can't sing."

"You sang," Giancarlo said positively. "And that was what loosened whatever hold he had on those kids. Before that, I could only have saved you with a blood bath."

"I'm sorry I was so stupid. I believed him when he said he had you. I really thought *I* was saving *you* by coming here."

His fingers stroked her hair over and over. It felt so good, so wonderful, considering she'd thought never to see him again.

"I'm a terrible cynic and a skeptic," he said low. "But I saw how you arrived. Did he lead you here? Was he in your head?"

She nodded, her hands clutching at his shoulders. "It was

so weird! It would have been funny, only... Later I might..."

"I was going to shoot him," Giancarlo said, "so he'd never get in your head again. Only the moment never came, and now it never will. Even for you, I can't kill a man in cold blood."

Via shuddered. "It doesn't matter. Giancarlo?" She caught his head between her hands until he looked into her eyes. His own were huge and black with anxiety for her, with guilt and with the echo of his old fear. "It doesn't matter," she repeated. "Letting him in like that taught me how to keep him out. Alive or dead, in prison or out, he'll never get to me that way again."

"Oh, it'll be prison," Giancarlo said grimly. "We've got him on your attempted murder, and with him in prison, it's only a matter of time until one of the kids, or all of them, tells the truth."

"Good." She shivered again. "He has power, though. Did you not feel it? Did you see the lightning? That was *him*!"

Giancarlo smiled. It was an odd little smile, with awe and uncertainty in there along with the admiration.

"Did you see the lightning stop?" he returned. "That was *you*."

It was already dawn by the time they got home to the blue house. Via and Giancarlo sat in the window seat at the top of the tower and watched the sun rise over the sea. To Via it was acknowledging a new beginning, a new life with the new gifts she could feel bursting inside her. A more practical plan was forming, too, of a new career that opened possibilities. And Giancarlo, Giancarlo... His name still rang like a song in her head, in her heart. The big, immovable yet oh-so-vulnerable man who was hers...

With her newfound confidence, she recognized that the chemistry between them ran deep and through both sets of veins. They were meant to be together, and Giancarlo knew it, too. Perversely, that was why he'd fought so hard against it.

Abruptly, she said, "He asked me what my price would have been. What it would take for me to join them. He even offered to cure you if I co-operated."

There was a pause, then: "Did you believe him?"

Via shook her head. "No. But it made me think. When does it stop being wrong?"

"When you take one life without permission for another of your own choosing."

His calm words soothed and dissipated all her doubts. She snuggled into him. "You've got it all sussed, haven't you?"

"Haven't you?" He lifted her chin so he could look into her eyes. "Were you tempted?"

"Yes," she said simply. "If...if you had been his prisoner, if I could really have saved your life by ending my own without a struggle, I think I would have done it."

"Oh, Via..."

"Only there would have been the other lives...and maybe I would have had the strength to do the right thing. When I'd worked out what it was."

Dipping his head so their foreheads touched, he said, "You need some sleep."

"I feel I'll never sleep again."

"Yes, you will. The sleep of the just."

She pulled her head back to look at him again. "Will you stay with me?"

His eyes closed. "Oh, don't tempt me! Sweetheart, we both need rest and we wouldn't get it squashed in that little bed. I'm afraid I'd make sure of it."

Watching the expressions flit across his face, Via understood and, almost to her own surprise, felt warmed by it. Confessing honestly to needing rest, and so by implication to the aftereffects of severe illness, was surely a breakthrough for him. Suppressing her own disappointment, she only smiled and agreed. "I suppose your mother wouldn't like it, either."

"I suppose she wouldn't. But maybe tomorrow, or later today, I suppose I mean, we can go back to Pisa? To your flat or mine."

The glint was back in his eye, tired but distinct, making her heart turn over and warming everything beneath.

"Yes, please," she said breathlessly, and opened her lips for his kiss.

As once before, he left her at her bedroom door with another rather too carefully passionless kiss, and so Via closed the door on him and prepared at last, slowly, for bed.

She woke with a start, aware of her heart drumming in her breast. Even through the closed shutters she could feel the heat of the afternoon sun. She was drenched in sweat. Dragging her unsteady hand across her face, she sat up and swung her feet onto the floor.

It hadn't been a terribly restful sleep, and she knew why. The dreams. Once she'd found it frustrating that she could never remember them, that all she ever had was the déjà vu when they came true. Now she thought that ignorance might have been a blessing. Because now, she did remember.

All the ills of the world. Or at least some of them, big and small. Other events, happy and sad, happening to people she didn't recognize. And some to people she did. Giancarlo, for example. She'd dreamed a lot of him—some plain silly, ordinary dreams that spoke of her obsession, her love, but others had been Those Dreams, visions, Sight, whatever she was supposed to call it. She felt, she *knew* the difference between them.

Yet no matter how much she tried to convince herself that the vision of Giancarlo making love to Angelina was just the ordinary dream laughing at her jealousy, she knew it wasn't true.

She stood, padded over to the window and threw open the shutters, grateful for the tiny gust of fresh air before the sun overwhelmed her.

She'd seen them twice together. Once Angelina had been wearing the same bright yellow trouser suit Via remembered, standing locked in Giancarlo's embrace. Once they'd been in bed, wearing nothing at all, joined together in some very imaginative and sweaty positions that obviously gave them both extreme pleasure.

Jealousy, inadequacy, twisted through Via like a knife. She was prepared to fight for Giancarlo, but God, how could she compete with Angelina? More beautiful, far more sexually experienced...

Despair and misery threatened to overwhelm her on this day that should have been her joy. With Marinuzzi in prison and Giancarlo her lover, they were about to return to Pisa to enjoy many days alone together before reality and the future stole in.

Seizing her towel and toiletries, Via left the room and headed for the shower. While the water cascaded over her body, she grew gradually calmer. Giancarlo didn't love Angelina—he'd said so, and she believed him. They'd outgrown each other, and now his feelings centered on Via. She knew that, too. She felt that. For the first time, she tried to think about the nature of these visions, about how they actually related to the future. Could what she saw be just one possible future?

Of course! Suddenly the idea that everything was already immovably mapped out for all eternity seemed both repugnant and senseless. All the things she saw—the floods, the killings, the famines, the marriages and births—they were merely possibilities. Giancarlo and Angelina were merely possible, and a possibility, surely, that had already passed. If it hadn't, then Via would take damned good care that it soon did.

Happier now, she padded back to her room. She could hear the sounds of talk and laughter downstairs. It was a happy house, she recognized, smiling. Giancarlo had a good family—she liked them, would enjoy being part of them.

Finally dressed in a loose cotton sundress, Via wandered to the window as she combed out her hair. Happiness had seeped back into her view of the world. She could admire the beauty of the hills and the sea, enjoy the warmth of the sunshine and the sweet smells of cut grass and lemon and herbs rising up from the garden. Giancarlo's father passed under the window, whistling as he stooped to pull a weed out of the garden. Straightening, he called something in the direction of the kitchen.

There was an extra car in the drive, parked in front of Giancarlo's. A very flashy, yellow sports car. It seemed the family had visitors. Humming to herself, Via wandered back into the room. She paused briefly to check her reflection in the mirror—she had to admit she looked not bad at all these days, with the glow of the Italian sun about her skin—before she went downstairs and, as Giancarlo had advised on her arrival, followed the noise toward the kitchen.

She wore her light, flat sandals. They made little sound on the carpeted stairs or on the hall floor which was covered by a big, Persian-style rug. The couple in the living room doorway clearly didn't hear her at all.

Angelina was dressed in yellow. And she was held tight in Giancarlo's arms. Her own arms were thrown around his neck, her eyes closed with some deep emotion as she pressed her cheek into his shoulder.

Via stood frozen before this tableau. It was so exactly what she'd dreamed that it took her breath away. It took everything away. The world, her bright, beautiful world of new love and excitement, crumbled and fell about her. She could almost hear the pieces shatter on the floor.

It seemed Angelina heard them, too, for her eyes suddenly opened straight into Via's. Their expression of horror and total guilt—and behind it, surely, laughter?—removed any last vestiges of doubt.

Feeling the sudden movement, Giancarlo released the woman in his arms and turned his head.

"Via."

Via was incapable of analyzing the expression in his voice or his unfathomable, dark eyes. She realized she always had been. A fool. Marinuzzi was right. Still a trusting fool. She'd built everything on nothing, and now she had to pay the price.

Somehow she managed to make her lips smile, made them part enough to speak.

"*Ciao*, Giancarlo," she whispered.

"What was that all about?"

His voice spoke from the bedroom door, which she hadn't even heard opening. Though it made her jump, she didn't turn to face him. Instead, she threw the last of her underwear into the bag on the bed and reached for the orange dress.

"Come to that," Giancarlo said slowly, "what is *this* all about?"

She felt him standing near her. Staring blindly at the scrunched up dress, she shoved it into the bag, too.

"It's about fidelity," she said, with barely a shake in her voice. "It's about what we can live with, and I've just discovered where my line is drawn. I can take a lot from you, Giancarlo. I can live with your moods and your stubbornness. I could even live with your illness if I had to. I could live with competition if that was all...but I can't share you. That's where *I* get off."

"Via, it was a hug."

His hands grasped her shoulders. Her eyes squeezed shut. *Don't touch me. I can't bear it if you touch me...*

She tried to shrug him off, but, relentlessly, he turned her to face him. She stood rigid in his hold, feeling his shock, his bewilderment wash over her.

"Via..." His fingers brushed at the wetness of her face, but the deluge kept coming, flooding from under her squeezed-shut eyelids to soak her face and hair and roll down her neck. "It was a hug from an old friend. You can't believe it was anything else."

"I can," Via whispered. "I can believe that."

"Because she was my wife? Not for ten years! We wouldn't have each other back now at..."

"Not because she was your wife," Via interrupted. "Because I *saw* it. I dreamed it."

Giancarlo's hands fell away from her shoulders. The cold sensation of loss made her feel even worse. Angrily, she dashed her arm across her wet face, digging her wrists into her eyes.

"What did you see?" Giancarlo asked evenly.

Via drew in her breath and looked at last into his face. It was veiled, as it had been yesterday when they'd talked about her psychic abilities. Before he'd seen it was the truth. Was he really doubting her again? At the very least, he was uncomfortable with her gifts.

"I saw you making love to Angelina."

His lips twisted into a smile. "That isn't Sight, Via, that's jealousy, and it's quite normal. I haven't made love to Angelina for rather more than ten years. She wouldn't let me, and I don't want to."

"What, never? You've never wanted her, not once in those ten years? You never even thought of it?" God, she sounded like a suspicious wife already...

Giancarlo shrugged impatiently. "Not seriously. I suppose it crossed my mind once or twice when I was feeling particularly randy. I thought of her and other ex-lovers. There's no big deal in that. Via, if we're together, I don't even need to *imagine* anyone else—and correct me if I'm wrong, but I believe we *are* together."

She stared up at him, anxious, desperate to be convinced. "Are we?" she whispered.

He didn't touch her, but his eyes grew warm, melting her cold fear. "There's a particular tree in the woods up there that can testify to that."

An involuntary laugh choked out. Heat flooded down from her tingling stomach to settle between her legs. And he was right. She was condemning him for something he hadn't done. At least not yet...

Ready to discuss it reasonably now, she said, "It *was* Sight, though. I can tell the difference."

Giancarlo frowned. "Well, maybe it was a past Sight. Maybe it was one future possibility we've already pushed aside by being together."

Stung by his impatience, she said, "I considered that."

"Then why all this drama?"

"Because of the *other* vision," she blurted.

Giancarlo cast his eyes to the ceiling. "The *other* vision," he repeated with exaggerated patience.

"Exactly! The one that came true! The one with you and Angelina hugging, just like downstairs."

"Oh, for the love of Christ, I *often* hug Angelina. My friends hug *me*. We're not *British*, for God's sake."

It might have been funny. Via might even have laughed, except for the genuine irritation in his voice. For a moment, she stared at him. Then, in a small, hard tone, she insisted, "It was my vision. *Exactly* my vision."

"Then you've no need to worry, have you? Because it was an innocent hug, not a torrid fuck. I won't alter my friendships to suit your visions. And you'd better understand, too, that we can't live our lives around them, either."

The hurt of that seemed to blast her backward. She actually took an involuntary step away from him, for his eyes were deadly serious. It wasn't just the harsh words. It was the annoyance behind them, the lack of understanding she'd never expected from him.

"Maybe *you* can't," she whispered. "But *I* have to."

"No, you don't." His voice softened. "In fact, you mustn't. You'll tie yourself in knots for nothing. Like you just have."

"For *nothing*?" She stared at him. "It happened!"

"So everything you dream must happen, too?"

Whirling away from him, she waved one deprecating arm. "I don't know. Maybe..."

"No," he said with certainty. "We can't live like that."

"You mean *you* can't," she flung over her shoulder.

There was a pause. It went on a long time. Via felt her heart break all over again. Slowly, she turned back to face him. His eyes were serious, intense, determined to make her understand. And Via thought she did.

"That's right," he said evenly. "I can't."

Curiously, it was easy this time, as if she'd done it before. When she spoke, her voice barely shook at all.

"Then will you phone me a taxi? I'm going back to Pisa."

Chapter Fourteen

As the train pulled out of the familiar tunnel into Aberton Station, Via felt a faint tingle of dread in her stomach. It almost pleased her, just because it seemed so long since she'd felt anything other than total misery. Perhaps she should have done it sooner, she reflected, standing with her overnight bag and going to the door. After all, if it was emotion she wanted, going home did it for her every time.

Except that it was emotion she'd been avoiding. There was just too much of it clogging her up, shutting down everything else but basic survival. So, although she'd been back in Scotland for a month, this was her first visit to Aberton—and for a Welcome Home party of all things. For herself.

She stepped off the train, walked up the steps and over the footbridge, just as she'd done a thousand times before. The evening was clear and bright, although the sharp east coast wind still whipped through her jacket, making her shiver.

She hadn't even told her brothers she was back. Every so often she sent them text messages from her phone to say she was okay, pretending to still be in Italy. Instead, she'd stayed in Edinburgh with her old flat-mate. She spent some time with another old friend, Peter, who'd put her in touch with others who could help her come to terms with her newly discovered "gifts". She'd learned to live with the dreams by seeing them as a vast array of past, present and future that was impossible to analyze, let alone pin down to certainty. She'd learned what to look for in case of the rare chance there was something she could and should try to influence. And she was learning to experiment with the use and control of her other mental gifts, receiving and sending telepathic thoughts. And hiding them.

It was a lot to occupy her mind. Yet at the same time, she'd enrolled in a college to learn to teach English as a foreign language. The same ability that had enabled her to pick up Italian so quickly enabled her now to see the patterns in English and to understand how to teach them. Her tutors said she was a natural, and since there was more practical speech than reading and writing involved, it worked perfectly for her. She'd found a promising and fulfilling new career. She was a gifted person. All the things she'd once longed for, before she went to Italy.

Perhaps in time she would learn to enjoy them. For now, she could barely live with her sense of loss, with the huge emptiness inside her.

Via took the path along the braes, as she nearly always did, letting in the sea view she'd known since childhood. In the gathering dusk, it lacked the dramatic color of the Tuscan coast, the sweeping, spectacular beauty, but on a smaller scale it held its own charm, and for no reason it brought a lump to Via's throat.

Turning away from the sea, she followed the lane up to the street and turned left. She could see it now, the house she was born in, a small, two-story cottage. Not for the first time since leaving home, she wondered how they'd all fitted in. Seven kids!

The lights were on all over the house. There were balloons tied to the gate. God, they'd really gone to town over this, as if she'd been away two years instead of two months. Her heart sank further.

Already, she could hear the music blaring out of the open windows. There were unlikely to be complaints, however, since most of the street would be in there. Almost involuntarily, her eyes strayed farther down the road, to the big detached house where Nico lived. Where it had all begun, she supposed, with Nico telling her about employment with Marinuzzi. And now he'd brought her home again.

Only now, she was wiser and far stronger than Nico could ever have imagined when he first sent her to Marinuzzi. She doubted it would enter his head that she'd come to confront him.

She began to drag her steps. She didn't want to go in, play a part, be happy and say how wonderful Italy was. She didn't want to be babied by her big brothers when she felt a woman for the first time in her life.

Get it over with, Via. Get in there.

Taking a deep breath, she turned in the gate, pushing balloons out of her face as she went. The front door was open. Carol, her oldest sister-in-law who'd never been good enough for Jim, stood there with her back against the wall, wearing her favorite little black dress and chatting to the young couple from across the road, glass in one hand, cigarette in the other. She and Via had never got on. Their eyes met.

Unexpectedly Carol smiled, pushing herself off the wall to say, "You got here then? Never thought you'd make it."

"I nearly didn't," Via confessed.

"Here, give me your bag and go and get a drink."

Well, Carol might not be good enough for Jim—who was, after all?—but she was all right. Better than the bitch who dumped Joe.

Via gave her a rueful smile with the bag and went single-mindedly in search of the booze. From experience, she knew it would be in the kitchen, which was inevitably stuffed full of people. *Why do people congregate in kitchens at parties? Because that's where the drink is, of course.*

Head down, Via eased her way in, hoping at least to get a glass in her hand before she was recognized. With any luck all these people were city friends of Joe and Davie and wouldn't know her from Adam.

"Via!"

Well, they might have been, but that was definitely Joe's voice, and Joe's bear-hug, and there was Davie, too, with Eileen, who must have forgiven him his lapse in fidelity. Via was surprised how much that relieved her. Underneath, she must have been worrying about them all the time, even while fixating on her own problems.

Joe's cheer echoed round the house and was taken up in every room. Via was hugged and squeezed and pushed into the living room for more hugs and shouts. They were all there, all six of them, and Jim's oldest daughter Amy, who looked far too grown up. Old friends and neighbors she'd known most of her life were grinning and welcoming her back. Stunned as she was, she couldn't help laughing with embarrassed pleasure. The uncompromising welcome wrapped a little warmth about her bruised heart, threatening her with an emotion she didn't think she was ready to bear yet.

Someone pushed her down onto the sofa. Terry demanded, "So what was it like, then? What's your favorite bit?"

And Amy asked, "Can you speak any Italian? What's Italian for...?"

"Has anyone given that poor lassie a drink yet?" Carol demanded, and Via blessed her silently amid the laughter—

prematurely, as it turned out. A glass of red wine extended through the throng, which parted good-naturedly to let the donor through. Smiling her fervent gratitude, Via reached for the glass—and looked into the serious, intense brown eyes of Giancarlo Di Ripoli.

The smile froze on her lips. The blood drained from her face so fast she thought she would faint. Shaking her head to clear it, she blinked, but when she opened her eyes, he was still there.

He pushed the glass into her hand, and her fingers closed automatically to hold it.

Via didn't know what to say, how to look away. He seemed just the same, with his smooth, shaven head and his cleanly sculpted face with its deeply etched crow's feet, though perhaps without that smile in his eyes. He wore blue jeans that hugged his hips, and a loose grey sweater.

Via couldn't breathe. Her heart thudded so loudly she couldn't even hear the rock music.

"An old friend for you, Via," Davie said with a wink, and amid the annoyingly ribald laughter, conversation started back up again.

Since everyone else had stood to greet her, Via was the only one sitting. Giancarlo dropped into the seat beside her and, immediately panicked, Via jumped up again. He caught her hand. At the touch of his fingers, her skin exploded in a million tiny sparks. Paralyzed by his effect on her, she gave in to the insistent tug and sat back down beside him.

"Via," he said low, just as he had the day she'd left him.

Her eyes closed. "Giancarlo, don't do this to me now," she whispered. "I can't do this now, I have to..."

"Have to what?"

"The world didn't stop when I left Italy." *Didn't it?* "I have other things on my mind right now."

When she plucked up the courage to glare at him again, she found him watching her with something like the same, steady focus of that first night in the hotel bar when she'd told him about her ordeal. Her stomach twisted. *It's only memory—I* won't *want him again...*

He said, "Things like long-postponed family reunions? Or—unfinished business?"

She frowned. "What do you mean?"

"I mean your neighbour who introduced you to Marinuzzi."

Incongruous to hear that name here. He belonged to a very distant world, like the man who sat beside her

He said quietly, "I'm here to help."

Of course. He'd come for Nico, too. He was working. If he'd really wanted her, he wouldn't have let her leave Italy. She knew that. She'd spent a month coming to terms with it just in case he ever contacted her again.

So why was this new excitement raging through her, filling her with life and hope where just moments ago there'd only been emptiness?

His thumb stroked her palm, sending shivers all the way up her arm and back down her spine. He said softly, "Later, we'll talk."

Via snatched her hand free. "There's nothing to talk to about. If there was, you'd have done it sooner."

He smiled slightly. For the first time, it was reflected in his eyes, though ruefully. "Via, it was you who ran away in a taxi."

She dropped her gaze. The temptation was to drown in his eyes. "You knew where to find me," she muttered.

"I let myself be persuaded you needed time to think."

"Persuaded by whom?" she demanded. "Angelina?"

"Yes," he admitted. "And Lisa and my mother, all of whose advice on women I have to value. To be honest, I was quite pitifully unsure of you. But I should have realized..."

"Realized what?" She wished she had the strength just to walk away.

"That I knew *you* as they didn't. I should have trusted my instincts. I drove to Pisa the next morning, went to your apartment, but you'd already gone. I even hung around the airport."

There was no denying this confession eased a little of her hurt, restored a modicum of pride. But if he thought that was enough, if he thought that was *nearly* enough...

"With Angelina?" she asked with savage civility.

"No. There's nothing between Angelina and me except a very long friendship. What upset you was only her wishing me well because of *you*."

"Then why did she look guilty as hell?"

"Because she knew you would misunderstand, as you did. Because *she* had messed it up this time when she'd been telling me off for doing so before."

Slowly, because she couldn't help it, Via's gaze came back to him. It wasn't everything, but it was something and, miserably, she knew she wanted to pursue it further, to make it more. She desperately wanted him to explain away the month of silence, not least because she didn't want to think of him as a man who took a month of her heartache to make up his mind. That would mean she'd misjudged him, had misjudged everything.

However much of this was mirrored in her helpless gaze, it was enough to soften his dark eyes. They grew suddenly warm—surely—*hopeful?* His hand rose, cupping her cheek in a quick gesture of tenderness that she had to force herself not to snuggle into.

"Giancarlo..." she began, then, almost like a needle point, she felt someone's sharp observation. Her gaze flew beyond Giancarlo to the living room door, and there, watching them from among the throng in the hall, stood the bent, elderly figure of Nico.

Giancarlo's hand fell away from her, leaving her face cold in the overheated house. He turned casually to follow her gaze. By this time, Nico was moving into the room. Dressed informally, for him, in creased cotton trousers and open-necked shirt, he was followed by his plump, smiling wife. Via tried to force her brain to think, to warn Giancarlo who it was she was going to introduce. But his quick squeeze of his fingers on hers told her he already knew. Without special "gifts", they could still communicate.

Registering the warmth of that, she realized further that the dread had gone from her stomach. Giancarlo was back, even if just for the night.

Smiling with as much sincerity as she could muster, Via rose to take both of Nico's outstretched hands.

"Via! How wonderful to see you back."

Via muttered something trite and friendly and turned with relief to greet his wife. Then, before she could introduce Giancarlo, she saw Nico hold his hand out to him.

"And you must be Via's Italian friend," he said in his own language.

Giancarlo smiled lazily, talking the offered hand and shaking it. "How did you guess?"

Nico laughed, a full, joyous sound that had never sounded remotely sinister to Via before. "Who but an Italian would wear a sweater to a party on a Scottish summer night?" He indicated his own light garb. "As you see, I have grown acclimatized over the years."

Although Via thought it would be impossible to behave with anything like normality at this party—not only was there Nico to worry about, but the unexpected presence of Giancarlo to churn her up all over again—it was surprising how quickly she fell back into the swing of things. In spite of all her confused emotions, she found herself ridiculously pleased to see her brothers again, and the rest of the family. She was genuinely interested in the latest happenings with her old friends and neighbors, and somehow the evening flew by. Behind it all, even when he wasn't with her, lay the burning, tingling pleasure of Giancarlo's nearness, the possibilities of which she wouldn't even consider. All she knew was that he dangerously outshone Nico in importance.

And yet she barely saw him, let alone spoke to him. She glimpsed him once with Joe and his friends, who were all laughing uproariously at something Giancarlo had said, and the urge to listen in, to join them, tugged at her so hard she had to flee to the toilet to fight it.

Splashing cold water onto her burning face, she wished she could cool her excitement as easily. *He hasn't come for you, he's come for Nico,* she told herself severely.

But he's here, he's here...

And he'll go again. If he'd really wanted you, he'd have been here a month ago. Face it, you pushed him into something he wasn't ready for, then freaked him completely with the psychic stuff.

But he's here. To look after me...

To finish the case. Nico's the last loose end.

Christ, why do I care? She scrubbed her face with the towel. *Because without him, I'm only half alive. Because one evening with him is more important than a lifetime with anyone else. When did I become so pathetic?*

Nico. Forget Giancarlo. Think Nico. One way or another, she needed to know if he'd deliberately sent her as a sacrifice to Marinuzzi. If Nico himself was involved in Satanic ritual and murder. Before she'd gone to Italy she'd have laughed to scorn anyone who'd come up with such a bizarre accusation. Now he seemed different. *She* was different.

It was time to seek him out. It was late enough. Everyone was drunk enough. If he really was what she believed him to be, he'd be ready to act. She could do this. All it would take was courage and a clear head.

When she emerged from the bathroom, Giancarlo stood on the landing outside, propping up the wall with his shoulder. Trying to ignore the lurch of her heart, she muttered, "Sorry—on you go," and brushed past him to the stairs.

"Actually, I was waiting for you."

She cast a skeptical glance over her shoulder, and his eyebrows quirked. "It seemed my only chance of catching you alone."

"Too late," she snapped, but before the words were finished, he'd leapt down in front of her, blocking her view of the guests below. Large, solid, immovable, more overwhelming than she remembered.

"Via. Let's do it differently this time."

Her heart galloped, but she was damned if she'd let him see it. "I'm not doing anything with you."

"Work together, you said."

She frowned. "What?"

"The night you drove to Marinuzzi to save me. You said we should work together, and I wouldn't. That's why we got into such hot water. Work with me now."

A choke of something not quite laughter caught in her throat. Not a plea to take him back after all. She should have known. But he was here. He was looking after her. And he was trusting her.

Without a word, she turned and walked back upstairs, away from the noise, past the bathroom and through the little hallway to the spiral stair that led to her tiny attic room. She didn't look back, but she knew he followed her.

Her overnight bag lay on the freshly made bed. *Thanks, Carol.* Via went to the window that overlooked the graveyard and the sea beyond. On another night five months ago, she'd stood here trying to keep hold of the dream of satanic murder.

The door closed with a quiet click. She could smell him. Some light cologne, some indefinable scent that was only Giancarlo. It wound through her senses, triggering memories and longings that she had to suppress if she was to achieve anything tonight.

She turned to face him.

He leaned against the closed door, watching her. She swallowed. "Are you here officially?"

He nodded. "I'm working with your local police. We're watching Nico and we're ready to act when he does."

"Then you believe he was actually in league with Marinuzzi?"

"A girl died here, too, you know. A tourist who inexplicably fell off the cliff to her death."

She'd had the same suspicion, but to hear him say it made it so much more real. She shivered. "Do you think he'll come after me?"

"He'll have heard what you did to Marinuzzi. He'll want your power, too, perhaps solely for himself, perhaps to try and help Marinuzzi. I think he'll come after you."

"I think so, too."

"Were you really going to take him on alone?"

She kicked at the base of her old bookcase. "I need it to be finished. I don't want anyone else hurt." And she couldn't imagine the local police buying the Satanism angle even though Giancarlo said he was working with them.

Giancarlo moved away from the door, glancing around the room as if taking it in for the first time—the untidy jumble of childhood toys and adult souvenirs, the Italian prints littering her walls revealing her long-standing obsession with his country, the tattered stuffed monkey on her narrow bed.

He said, "If you bait him, would you trust us to hook him?"

In truth, it lifted a huge weight from her. She had no idea of Nico's strength. She couldn't read him, but sensed a powerful block that boded ill for her in a mind-battle. Old-fashioned brute strength would be welcome.

She nodded, and a lopsided smile tugged at his mouth. "I'll follow but...do you have any idea where he would take you?"

She jerked her head toward the window. "Over there. They threw witches off the cliff in the sixteenth century. Or at least *one* witch."

"Where the other girl died. You think he'd risk us making the connection?"

"There's no connection with him. I'm sure he'll have an alibi prepared. But I don't know for certain. I'm only guessing."

"Wherever he takes you, we'll be watching. Via?"

He'd come to a halt directly in front of her. Too close, but she refused to step back. "What?"

"You don't have to do this."

"I do. There's no evidence against him, and he needs to be stopped before he harms anyone else."

"I won't let him hurt you."

And who'll stop you *hurting me?* Appalled, she felt tears strain at her throat. Swallowing them down, she said, "I know." It sounded too harsh, but it didn't repel him. Instead, he touched her cheek, butterfly light, threatening to undo her completely.

She flinched as though burned, and his hand fell away. He whispered, "I missed you."

Her eyes closed, blotting out the seductive yearning in his. "Bullshit. The remedy was in your own hands."

She stepped round him. "Let's get this over with. I'm going to talk to Nico."

She didn't wait for him, just pushed blindly out of the room and ran downstairs.

By now, the noise of the party was deafening to anybody not previously numbed by copious quantities of alcohol. Via had moved on to water after her first glass of wine. She hoped people would think it was gin, although some instinct prevented her from playing drunk.

Pausing only for a quick, laughing exchange with Eileen, her favorite sister-in-law, who was not, in fact, married to Davie but who earned the title of wife through sheer long suffering, Via went straight toward Nico's frail-looking back.

He stood chatting with some of the other neighbours but, as if he sensed her approach, he turned away from them and came to meet her, smiling.

Her heart began to beat harder because she knew this was it. She wondered if he could feel it.

"I was hoping to have a chat with you tonight, Via," he began, the apologetic look in his eyes surely genuine. "I can't tell you how sorry I am that my recommendation got you into so much trouble in Italy. I never dreamed Marinuzzi had changed so much. Completely mad, I hear..."

"Barking," she agreed lightly. "But don't blame yourself. I'm a big girl, and there's no harm done."

"I wish I could believe that."

Two of Joe's friends erupted out of the kitchen at that point, laughing loudly as they vied for the last can of their favorite beer. Via squeezed herself against the wall to let them past. One of them did a double-take, then paused, leaning into her with his beery breath.

"Via? Joe's wee sister?"

"That's me," she confessed.

"Wow, you've changed."

"At least you didn't say 'grown'. How's your wife, Jamie?"

Jamie laughed, realizing he'd been rumbled, and good-naturedly straightened. "She's fine. So are the twins. Nice to see you again." And he departed in search of other, less discerning prey.

"A party is not the best place to talk, after all," Nico remarked. He hesitated as Via smiled perfunctorily, then asked, "Do you want to take a quick walk, tell me about it in peace? I feel...responsible. I know that's what your mother would say, too."

Via's fists clenched. The glass in her hand nearly shattered. It took all of her newly learned control, but in the end she neither raged nor ran. Instead she said, "Okay. I'll just get my jacket."

Since they were in the hall, she didn't have far to go to pick her jacket off the banister. She risked a casual look around, but couldn't find Giancarlo. All she could see on the way out was the stocious figure of Joe's friend Jamie, burping loudly into his can, much to the entertainment of his pals.

"It looks as if he'll go home to Mrs. Jamie tonight after all," Nico said dryly, and in spite of herself Via laughed. Opening the gate, she went out into the street and turned left toward the beach.

"Where's Maria?" she asked a moment later, suddenly remembering Nico's wife.

"She went home a little while ago. Tired out."

Via just nodded. It was hard not to look back over her shoulder.

"So," Nico said after a short silence. "Your Italian friend—someone important?"

"Important, yes." No other words would come. She couldn't talk about Giancarlo to anyone, least of all to him.

He waited for more, but when it wasn't forthcoming, he only asked, "How did you meet?"

"He drove me home in a taxi," Via replied. "Listen, I think the local kids are having a party on the beach..."

Nico's kids? As Marinuzzi had had his? So far, it didn't sound like it. There was no chanting, only undisciplined, erratic yelling and laughing. Just teenagers with too much beer and alcopop.

Confirming it, Nico said, "Saturday night—too many parties. Let's go this way instead. We can look at the sea from the cliff top."

And he crossed the road with his slightly bent yet still

distinguished gait, leading her onto the side road. She'd been right. They were going to the graveyard.

Nico asked, "Do you think Marinuzzi picked you deliberately?"

"That's funny. The Italian police asked me the same thing."

"What did you say?"

"I said there was nothing special to pick on me *for,* except that I was alone in a foreign country and couldn't speak the language."

"Seventh child of a seventh child," Nico murmured, wandering off the pavement and into the graveyard. Via followed him across the shadows of the gravestones looming on both sides.

"Meaning what?" she asked, allowing scorn into her voice.

Nico smiled. He seemed in no hurry to answer. The look of frailty had vanished from his straight, fit body. Via had always admired the vitality and intelligence that gleamed in his direct, dark eyes. Now, in the pallor of the patchy moonlight, they glittered. She'd always sensed there was more to him, had liked him for it. Now she wondered if he'd *made* her like him. For, studied dispassionately, his face bore very little sign of the gentle, retired businessman he liked to portray. It looked hard, thin-lipped, uncompromising and far younger than his sixty-odd years. At the party, he'd seemed much older.

He strolled onward toward the back of the cemetery where a fence lined the cliff top. There, at the edge of the promontory, some poor woman had been put to death as a witch four hundred years ago.

It was darker here where the streetlights didn't penetrate, and the sea was louder, rushing and swirling over the rocks below. Via kept pace with him, trying to calm the beating of her heart, trying to concentrate on Nico and not on the whereabouts of Giancarlo. She wondered if he had backup, wished she'd asked the right questions. Wished she'd said goodbye before she left the house. If nothing else, she would know he was aware of her going.

Nico spoke at last, answering the question she'd forgotten she'd asked. "Meaning it makes you valuable to people in search of...gifts. I think you have gifts, Via."

Her heart lurched, threatening to unsteady her voice. "What gifts?" she demanded.

"Latent ones. Seeing, definitely, from what I heard from your mother and brothers."

"So why try to kill me? My so-called 'gifts' wouldn't be much use then."

"An adept could absorb them at the moment of sacrifice."

Via leaned her arms against the fence and peered over it at the grey sea. Despite the noise it made, it looked quite still, not crashing but rippling very gently on to the rocks below her. A long way down.

"An adept what?" she mocked, playing her part, determined not to rush him just to get this over with.

"An adept Satanist."

She let herself turn to stare at him now. His stance was quite casual, both hands in his trouser pockets. But he was watching *her* in the darkness, not the view, and there was nothing remotely casual about his gaze, bright and sharp in his lined, lived-in face.

So it's to be now, then. All right, let's go for it.

"How do you know so much about it?"

"Because, my dear, I *am* one. I sent you to Marinuzzi. As a gift."

There was no remorse, no friendliness in his gaze, no sign

of the amiable neighbour she'd known so long. Through the darkness he appeared, if anything, amused. It was the amusement that did it. That and the word "gift". Suddenly, she wasn't afraid at all.

She said, "I know you did, Nico. That's why I came home—to see you."

A frown twitched Nico's brow, freezing his face for the barest instant before he laughed.

"Via, Via, have you understood nothing even yet? I'm not what you think. I've never been what you think. You cannot *reason* with me."

"I know," she acknowledged. "But I didn't come for a heart to heart. I came to make sure."

His expression was almost admiring. "Brave," he mocked. "But foolhardy."

"You think so? When everyone saw you leaving with me a few minutes ago?"

He only smiled at that. "My dear, no one will remember seeing us leave. Besides, I'm getting old. And actually you'll find—or at least *you* won't, though others will—that several people will remember seeing *me* in the pub at around this time."

For some reason that chilled her more than anything else. "You can do that?" she whispered. "Plant false thoughts and memories in people's minds?"

"Easily, my dear. As you'll find out yourself, in just a moment. How do you imagine it was that no one saw me walking through the town with that poor little English tourist who fell to her death in 2002? She threw herself over the railing—just here—without a murmur of protest, I assure you. I am, you see, twice as powerful as Marinuzzi."

"Rather more than that, I should think," Via murmured,

remembering her last image of Marinuzzi, slumped and bewildered in the hands of the police. Nico frowned again, taking a step nearer as he peered into her face. Her heart drummed unpleasantly, but she forced her body to stay still.

"I should thank you for the compliment," he observed, "only something tells me it wasn't meant as such."

"Oh, no," she agreed. "Didn't you know Marinuzzi and both his sons will stand trial for murder?"

Nico waved that aside. "We'll see. Or at least, I will. But you, your trauma in Italy, the guilt of framing a decent man like Marinuzzi, will clearly prove too much for you. You take your own life. Now be a good girl and climb up there on the wall for me."

She was prepared for it. Yet even so the force of his coercion blasted her across the rough ground. It was instinct to fight back, and she did, not with the new control she'd been learning over the last month, but with blind, intuitive fury, an animal determination to survive. As soon as she hit the wall, she used it as an anchor, a base from which to hold tight and hurl her mind like a knife into his.

Via meant to hurt, to fight as powerfully as she could, but even she was taken by surprise when Nico fell like a stone, screaming and clutching his head. Startled, she nearly let go, but some old fear, some distrust mixed with sheer anger, made her keep the knife there. She could feel his agony, his terror and, finally, glowing like the eyes of some malevolent beast, his power. Twisting the psychic knife, she advanced on the power, physically walking forward until she stood over him, digging, rooting, throwing away.

"The Devil did not give you this power," she whispered, lost in the sheer horror and grief of her task. "Some people just *have* it, some don't. You and Marinuzzi, you simply *learned* from the people you killed. Your feeble telepathy picked up from theirs. But you were so obsessed with those stupid Satanist fantasies that you learned from *children*, for God's sake. You were too weak, too greedy to understand. You didn't need to kill them. They didn't need to die..."

Abruptly, a hand on her shoulder pulled her backward. Wrenched out of Nico's mind, she only just prevented herself from attacking the newcomer with equal ferocity. Instead, she tried to pull free physically, twisting in the hold of a man. A man in a woolen sweater and a leather jacket. In summer.

"Giancarlo," she whispered, racked in anguish. She reached up to clutch the offending sweater with both hands. Tears poured down her cheeks. "He didn't need to kill her. He didn't need to kill any of them!"

"I know, Via, it was never about need... It's all right now, shhh..." Giancarlo held her in both strong arms, soothing her like a baby, his cheek on the top of her head until she quieted. Twisting her face into the sweater to wipe away the wetness, she could make out beyond his shoulder the straight, poised figure of Joe's friend Jamie. Even in the dark, striding over to Nico, he showed no signs of the drunkenness which had debilitated him only half an hour earlier. The Satanist was still curled, whimpering, on the ground.

Giancarlo let her go and moved with Jamie. Bending, he yanked Nico's hands downward, twisting them behind his back while he rolled and bucked on the earth. Jamie got the handcuffs on him. Nico lay still.

Via advanced upon him and looked down into his blank, vacant eyes. He was an old man, wounded and pitiful.

"Christ," she whispered. "What have I done?"

Giancarlo grabbed him by the chin, and the eyes swiveled to find him, curiously out of focus. "Given him the equivalent of a knock-out punch, I think. He'll be fine, unfortunately."

Not quite fine, Via realized. Not quite. She could root around in Nico's mind freely now and she did, briefly, before withdrawing in distaste. Whatever powers he'd possessed she'd cleared out for good.

But Giancarlo was still looking at her, a faint, heartrending smile on his lips. "You really don't need me at all, do you?"

Chapter Fifteen

Via stared at him, reeling. "*Need* you? I *hurt* with need, I am *dying* with..." She slumped back against the fence, fighting to control the emotion that swamped her, to keep the words inside. "Christ, there's more to life than this *mess*."

She dragged her shaking hand across her face, so she didn't see him move. But she felt him grasp her shoulders, his hands heavy and urgent. She gave a strangled sob, raising her arms to push him away then dropping them with a sort of furious helplessness. The flashing light from an approaching police car lit his intense face.

"Via, do you love me?"

Her eyes closed. Oh, no, this wasn't fair! *Strong. You're strong, remember?*

She opened them again, straight into his. "I don't change with the weather. But I won't spend the rest of my life chasing you when you couldn't even come to Pisa to find me."

"I came to Pisa for you."

"The next day. And then what? You lost my number? You couldn't get on a bloody plane?"

She hadn't meant to say the last bit. She didn't want him to know how badly she'd needed him to follow. Just for once, she'd wanted to be the pursued.

His intense brown eyes stared into hers. The words seemed to stick in his throat, and she was fiercely, ill-naturedly glad to have made this difficult for him. His upper teeth closed over his lower lip and let it go.

He said, "Actually, no, I couldn't get on a bloody plane. Not that day. Because the following day was my check-up at the hospital."

Oh, Christ! Oh Jesus, Jesus, please!

She swallowed. "What did they say?" The words came out as a whisper. No wonder he'd been so on edge, and she'd just pushed and pushed...

"They say I'm still clear and they don't want to see me for another year."

Her eyes closed again. She laid her forehead on his chest. She had no words. Beside this nothing else mattered, least of all her own pride. His arms slid right round her, drawing her into him. She pulled back her head to ask for more information and found her mouth seized by his. God, she'd dreamed of his kisses night and day over the last month. Even the strongest woman on Earth couldn't be expected to draw away now, not when her very bones were melting with relief and longing and increasingly heated desire.

As he quickly hardened against her, she felt the flooding release in her knickers and gasped. His tongue pushed against hers, exploring hungrily. He sucked her tongue into his own mouth, biting and caressing until she returned the kiss as fiercely with her own lips and tongue and teeth. His hands slid down her back, caressing her buttocks, pulling them so he could grind his erection into her.

"Giancarlo!"

The world rushed back with Jamie's call and, gasping, Via broke free of the kiss.

Nico, still stunned and docile, was being led to the police car. Via gave a watery laugh. "We've been here before, haven't we? Yet another déjà vu. Another country, another graveyard..."

"No," said Giancarlo. "No, it isn't. Via...?"

"What?" she demanded. His eyes burned her, thrilling her, frightening her with the strength of her own response. He drew in his breath.

"Wait. Just wait there." He strode away from her toward the police car where Jamie was grinning.

"Sorry to interrupt," she heard Joe's friend mock, and turned, staring instead at the rocks and sea below, where Nico had wanted to her jump, to break her own body and drown.

Via wanted to go back to the party and get absolutely wasted. No, she didn't. She wanted to go to bed with Giancarlo.

Her gaze strayed back to him. He nodded to Jamie, and both men moved toward her, leaving the police car to drive off. In the back seat, Nico sat staring straight ahead of him. Poor Maria...

"You all right, Via?" Jamie asked cheerfully.

"Fine."

"Well done. His threats came through loud and clear, and we should be able to get him for the tourist murder in 2002 as well. Sorry about the business back at the house, by the way. Wasn't sure you knew who I was, and I didn't want His Nibs there to suspect."

"I wasn't offended," Via assured him. "When did your twins arrive?"

Jamie grinned. "They haven't. Got no kids at all as yet. Just seemed too good a line to pass up. See you, Via."

"See you, Jamie."

She watched him saunter off, hands in pockets. Done and

dusted. Was that a tingle of relief she felt that this whole Marinuzzi business was finally finished? Barring any required court appearances, of course.

She pushed herself off the fence. “Want to go to a party?” she asked Giancarlo.

“No. I want to make love to you.”

Her heart lurched, flooding her with heat. She had a brief but spectacular vision of them falling together among the gravestones, of his naked body thrusting and straining inside her.

He took her in his arms, holding her close against his body. His cock was still rigid. Its heat burned her, toppled her desperate resolutions. She knew better than to let him kiss her again, but it seemed she couldn’t stop him, and God it was sweet to be hunted at last, to hold him...

He came up for breath, devouring her with his hot gaze.

“Christ, Via, where can we go?” he whispered, bending to capture her mouth again. It was as if he couldn’t get enough of her, and even with her own body on fire, she found time to rejoice in that.

“To my party,” she said against his lips. He smiled into her mouth.

“Don’t torture me. Don’t you have a bedroom there?”

“Yes, I do, but I can’t go to bed when there’s a party on.”

“Via...” He reached for another kiss, but she fended him off more forcefully this time.

“Oh no. You think because you’ve got the answer you wanted at the hospital that you can just pick me up now? Well, you can’t. What was the month between for? Dramatic effect?”

“No.” He hesitated, then said, “I bought my ticket here, then called in to work to arrange a return date. We’d been in touch with the police here, suspecting Nico's involvement and fearing for your safety now that you were home. We were also concerned about the tourist who died here so inexplicably a few years ago. I...I pulled some strings to come here as liaison. I don't know why I didn't phone. Mostly, I think, because I wanted to talk to you in person. And because I wanted you to have time to make up your mind about me, and about your new gifts. So I didn't phone. I just came."

"So, you've been here nearly a month and I didn't know?" What the hell use were psychic gifts anyway? "Where were you?"

"Watching Nico. And watching you," he confessed. "Waiting for Nico to make contact with you."

She frowned with suspicion. "I never saw you."

"I should hope not. I am well trained. I didn't contact you until now because if Nico knew I was here, perhaps saw us together and guessed what you meant to me, he might have acted before we were ready. Or done nothing at all until I'd gone. So I only introduced myself to your family today."

"Giancarlo, if you knew what I...how much I..."

He caught her in his arms again. "Forgive me," he whispered into her hair. "Forgive me, I am a stupid man, but I have been in my own hell. When you left, I was so afraid you'd discover what you felt for me wasn't real, just some passing, physical crush, because I was your first..."

Catching his head as he plunged for her mouth once more, she gasped, "No you don't. Wait. I want to know what will happen next time your check-up approaches. Next time you're worried about your health. I'm not *prepared* to be picked up and put down for that reason. If we fight, if we end it, we do so for *good* reasons. And you have to accept that my gifts are real, Giancarlo, *real*!"

"Agreed," he said breathlessly, his hands roaming up her sides, pausing at her breasts and moving inward. "And I know that your gifts are real, part of you. Perhaps we both needed a little time to adjust to that..."

Standing still in his arms, she let him caress her, let him feel her involuntary responses to his touch. His palms smoothed over her pebble-hard nipples before his fingers closed on them in a long, pulling caress.

It was all she could do not to moan aloud. She swallowed.

"Easy words. Prove it," she said softly, and brushed his hands away. She slipped out of his arms and began to walk toward the cemetery gate.

"How?" asked Giancarlo in her ear.

"That's up to you."

"And how exactly do you mean to fend me off in the meantime?"

"I have six brothers in the house, all staying the night."

"They like me."

"Not that much. Trust me."

His soft laughter tickled her neck an instant before his lips found it. Delicious pleasure rippled down her spine, but though her fists clenched then opened wide with the effort, she managed not to reach for him. Instead, she let him walk the rest of the way home with his arm around her waist. His fingers did show a sanity-threatening tendency to slip inside the band of her jeans to caress the skin of her stomach and hips, but she bore it bravely without comment.

Though the front door was still open, the music was quieter now, and the hall was empty. A few die-hards sat on the stairs drinking, including Jim and Davie who raised their beer bottles and grinned when Via and Giancarlo wandered in.

"Nice walk?" Davie asked.

"You'd be surprised," Via replied.

"No, he wouldn't," said Jim, and they all fell about laughing.

Rolling her eyes, Via walked into the living room. The sisters-in-law were there with Joe and Archie from next door, who was nearly asleep.

"Coffee?" Via suggested. "Tea?"

"I'll get it," Carol volunteered, surprisingly enough.

"Sit on your bum, woman, you've done enough for the evening," Via commanded and won another rare, if sleepy smile from her.

"Good girl. Your man there'll help you. Make a strong one for Archie," she added, tipping her head at the nodding, middle-aged man beside her.

She was very aware of Giancarlo following her into the empty kitchen. The place was like a bomb site. Bottles and plates and food covered every available surface.

"Shit," said Via, pushing a pile of bottles away from the kettle. Picking up a barely started wine bottle, she took a healthy slug and passed it to Giancarlo. For the first time since she'd known him, he took a swig of wine and laid the bottle down. His hands reached toward her, and her breath caught. But he only stretched behind her and picked up an empty bag. Quickly and efficiently, he began loading the bottles into the bag. It cleared one work top. That done, he pushed the door closed with his heel. Via, busying herself with tea pots and coffee pots, saw out of the corner of her eye that he picked up the old kitchen chair and wedged the back of it under the handle. Her heart beat furiously.

Reaching for the tea caddy, she saw his hand before she

felt it, closing over her breast. Instantly, her body melted into a helpless pulp. His free hand slid round to cup her other breast, drawing her back against him. Feebly, she opened her mouth to object and found it silenced under his. It was too much. Her mouth opened for him. She emitted a small, animal moan of pleasure and need as she reached blindly up behind her to touch his face.

Instantly, she felt his response. His mouth began to move on hers with fierce passion. One hand swept down her breast across her stomach to the wet, hot place between her legs. Her thighs parted for him without her permission, and his fingers kneaded and stroked her to wildness while she pressed herself back into his thrusting erection.

Twisting to face him, she flung both arms around his neck, kissing him, burrowing her hands under his sweater, desperate to feel the naked skin of his back and chest. He paused for an instant to pull off both the sweater and the shirt underneath, and she devoured his chest, licking and biting at his nipples. His fingers were at her zipper, tugging, pulling her jeans down over her hips to her thighs.

Via tried to make some incoherent objection. At once, he lifted her, swinging her round and setting her down on the cleared work top. Standing between her legs, he pressed his erection into her and pushed up her T-shirt, freeing her breasts with hands that trembled.

"Giancarlo, we can't! Someone might come in." God, her voice shook as well.

"They can't get in." His lips had hold of one nipple while his fingers caressed the other. His breath, the movement of his lips as he spoke, fired her with delight.

"They'll hear us."

"I don't care if you don't."

"My brothers will kill you."

"No, they won't. Let me in, Via, I want you so badly... I love you." On the last word he lifted his head, seizing her mouth once more in his so she couldn't respond. It took the last of her sanity. Tightening her arms around him, she gave him everything in her kiss. She fumbled with the fastening of his jeans until he did it for her, freeing his big, purple-headed cock.

Slowly, she lifted her gaze from his shaft, over his flat stomach and muscled chest, to his eyes. He nudged her once with his cock, seeking and finding position, then, deliberately, he pushed inside her.

Sensation exploded, so intense she couldn't deal with it. Her eyes closed.

"Look at me," he said fiercely. Surprised, she obeyed and remembered afresh the joy of seeing his eyes hot and clouded with passion for her, of watching every pleasure she gave him reflected in his face.

"Giancarlo," she whispered, taking his face between her hands. "Giancarlo..."

He began to move inside her with strong, sensual strokes, watching her avidly. Tilting her hips, she caressed him with the soft, moist walls of her pussy, pulling him into her while her hands roamed down his throat and chest and shoulders, reaching around his back. She couldn't get enough of him. Thrusting herself onto him as far as she could, she gasped out her delight, her need.

Seeming to sense her every desire, he increased the tempo, driving harder and faster until her desperate climax broke over her in wave after wave of wild, intense joy. She collapsed on his chest, her hips writhing, her ecstatic moans lost in his mouth as he gave one last fierce thrust and fell into his own orgasm. From deep in his chest came a low, growling series of gasps. Via kissed him harder as if trying to swallow them.

"Via!" Carol's voice came from the living room. "Where's that coffee?"

"It's coming," said Via breathlessly, then lower to Giancarlo, "Actually, it's all that isn't!"

He leaned against her, his sweaty chest heaving with laughter as well as exertion. She could feel the trembling of his legs. "God, I love you."

"Really?" she asked in a small voice.

"Yes, really." His fingers touched her cheek, butterfly-light. "I know I do things wrong sometimes, but really, I meant to keep a distance between us for the best of reasons. I truly don't want you tied to my sick bed."

"If you're sick, that's where I'll be. It's called love."

"No, this is love," he said, slowly withdrawing his still-hard cock from her, watching its languid progress.

"It's all part of the same thing. Whatever happens, good and bad, your issues and mine, promise me we'll do it together, for..." As his gaze came back up to hers, she changed the words. "For as long as we *are* together."

He smiled with a tenderness that melted her all over again. "Via," he said, resting his forehead on hers, "just call it 'forever'. We both know that's what it is."

About the Author

To learn more about Marie Treanor, please visit www.marietreanor.com. Send an email to Marie at marie@marietreanor.com or join her Yahoo! group to join in the fun with other readers as well as Marie. http://groups.yahoo.com/groupsexydelights. Subscribe to Marie's Newsletter:

http://groups.yahoo.com/marietreanornewsletter.

LaVergne, TN USA
27 October 2009
162203LV00002B/152/P

9 781605 044279